W9-AVY-353

STUART McLEAN

STORIES
FROM THE
VINYL CAFE

Stuart mclean

VIKING

VIKING
Published by the Penguin Group
Penguin Books Canada Ltd, 10 Alcorn Avenue, Toronto, Ontario, Canada
M4V 3B2
Penguin Books Ltd, 27 Wrights Lane, London W8 5TZ, England
Viking Penguin, a division of Penguin Books USA Inc., 375 Hudson Street,
New York, New York 10014, U.S.A.
Penguin Books Australia Ltd, Ringwood, Victoria, Australia
Penguin Books (NZ) Ltd, 182–190 Wairau Road, Auckland 10, New Zealand

Penguin Books Ltd, Registered Offices: Harmondsworth, Middlesex, England

First published 1995
1 3 5 7 9 10 8 6 4 2

Copyright © Stuart McLean, 1995

All rights reserved. Without limiting the rights under copyright reserved
above, no part of this publication may be reproduced, stored in or introduced
into a retrieval system, or transmitted in any form or by any means
(electronic, mechanical, photocopying, recording or otherwise), without
the prior written permission of both the copyright owner and the above
publisher of this book.

*Publisher's note: This book is a work of fiction. Names, characters, places and
incidents either are the product of the author's imagination or are used fictitiously,
and any resemblance to actual persons living or dead, events, or locales is entirely
coincidental.*

Printed and bound in Canada on acid free paper ⊖

Canadian Cataloguing in Publication Data

McLean, Stuart, 1948-
Stories from the vinyl cafe

Essays from the CBC radio program The Vinyl Cafe.
ISBN 0-670-86476-5

I. Title.

PS8575.L44S76 1995   C814'.54   C95-930589-0
PR9199.3.M35S76 1995

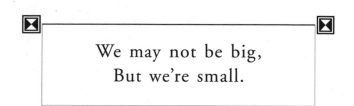

We may not be big,
But we're small.

Framed motto hanging
by the cash register
at The Vinyl Cafe

CONTENTS

STORIES

FROM THE

VINYL CAFE

THE PIG

The guinea pig was losing hair. Not shedding it, losing it. Morley said, "You better take her to the vet." Dave said to his wife, "I know."

The neighbourhood vet said she didn't do pigs. She told Dave he'd have to take her to a clinic that specialized in small animals. Dave wasn't sure how to move a sick pig across the city. He settled on the bus and a wooden fruit basket filled with wood chips. The pig didn't seem to mind the excursion. Neither did Dave.

The pig is Dave's job. He cleans her cage, he feeds her, and since she was sick he accepted that it was up to him to make her better. The pig is his son's pet, but when he bought her Dave knew that caring for her would eventually fall to him. He doesn't enjoy cleaning the cage two nights a week; often he resents it, but he never expected it to be any other way. The pig, after all, was his idea. Why shouldn't he look after her? Once it occurred to him that he did a better job caring for the guinea pig than he did for anyone else in his life—not that he cares for the pig more than his wife or kids— just that looking after her is clearer. He can see when her cage is dirty—and when it is, he knows what to do about it.

When he got to the vet a young receptionist asked him questions and typed his answers into her computer. When she asked for the pig's name Dave said, "Doesn't have a name."

Not liking the look that crossed her face he added, "We call her, The Pig…sometimes just Guinea." Dave, who has always felt naming animals was a questionable practice, thought naming a rodent was foolish and he hadn't encouraged the idea. But standing in front of the receptionist he felt shabby about owning an unnamed pig. As if that told her all she needed to know about him, and his family, and the way they cared for animals. As if it was suddenly obvious why the pig was sick.

Dave is foggy about the rest of the visit. But he can remember snatches of it. He remembers the receptionist ushering him into another room. He and the pig. He remembers he was left alone until another young woman walked in. In his memory she is wearing a white lab coat. She looks much too young to be a doctor, he thinks. When she plucks the pig out of its basket and holds her up confidently he thinks, Must be just out of school.

The young woman is asking him questions. She is poking the pig, petting her. She is taking her away. Dave waits in the front room—with the receptionist.

When the young vet, whose name was Dr. Hall, calls him back into the examining room she tells him that she suspects the pig has a tumour. Suspects. She couldn't be sure. Not without tests.

"We don't see a lot of guinea pigs," she adds.

Then she hands Dave a yellow piece of paper that he still has in his wallet. He has been showing it to every-one who lingers by the cash register at his store. At the top of the page it says:

ESTIMATE
GUINEA PIG—UNNAMED

What seized Dave's attention the moment Dr. Hall handed the estimate to him, and why he has been show-ing it around, is the figure at the bottom of the page.

ESTIMATE TOTAL: $563.30.
The ESTIMATE is carefully itemized:

Guinea pig examination and assessment	$37.00
4 days hospitalization exotic level 2	
@ $21.50/day	$86.00
Vitamin C injection	$12.00
Fluids, Reglan injection additional	
@ $6.00 each	$12.00
Exotic anesthesia induction fee	$30.00
20 mins. Isoflurane anesthesia	
@ $120/hr	$40.00
15 mins. Surgery minor category	
@ $200/hr	$49.95
Radiograph split plate	$62.00
CBC—done with profile	$25.00
Clinical chemistry 1 profile	$47.50
Cortisol (3 tests)	$75.00

Miscellaneous charges if needed
(medication at home, etc.) $50.00
7% GST to be added to final bill.
Estimated to be $36.85

The figure that galled Dave was the $21.50 a day for hospitalization. How could it cost $21.50 a day to feed and lodge a guinea pig? He himself had stayed in motels for less than $21.50 a night. How much could a guinea pig eat—especially after surgery?

At first he thought the estimate was a joke. Or maybe a mistake. Then he realized it was neither and he felt trapped. If he signed the estimate and handed the pig over to the vet he could imagine what they would have to say about him at closing time. What kind of person, he could hear the receptionist ask, would spend $500 on a guinea pig? A four-year-old sick guinea pig. A guinea pig that was going bald and could soon look like a worm with legs. A pig that was clearly playing on the back nine of pigdom. On the other hand, if he was to walk out, wouldn't that confirm everything that the receptionist had thought about him?

He asked if he could phone his wife. She wasn't home. I have to speak to my wife, he said, as he left with the pig. I'll phone you tomorrow.

Everyone he has asked says he did the right thing. Brian who opens the store Saturday mornings said so. Morley said so too. "Are you crazy?" she asked. At supper she made hair replacement jokes. She said if the pig lost all its hair she would knit her a little sweater.

His friend Al suggested he take the pig for a walk in the rain.

"That'll fix her," Al said.

Dave didn't try to explain what he was feeling. He knew it was crazy to spend $563.30 on a balding guinea pig that cost $30. But when you are standing in a vet's office holding a life in your hands it is easy to imagine yourself spending the money. It was after all a life. And it was, after all, in his hands.

The next evening after everyone else was in bed, Dave poured himself a beer and sat down at the kitchen table. He began writing a list of animals whose deaths he had already caused during his forty-five years of life.

1) One hamster. Not really his fault. She had died from chewing the wood in her cage. Dave's grandfather built the cage. And it was his grandfather who had painted it yellow. It was the lead in the paint that had killed the hamster. Dave remembers the night the hamster died. He remembers his mother feeding his hamster brandy from an eyedropper. What he can't remember is whether the hamster had a name.

2) Frogs. Too many to count. He had never actually killed a frog himself. But he had been present when frogs were killed. He must have been twelve when his friends had found the swamp. They went there and killed frogs in all sorts of fiendish ways. They stuck

straws up their asses and inflated them so they popped. They tied rocks to their legs and threw them into the water so they drowned. Dave remembers watching one frog, weighted down, its front legs pawing at the water, trying desperately to swim to the surface. He tried to remember whether he had said anything. Whether he had stood up for the frog or not.

Years later he went to Honolulu and toured the wreckage left from the attack on Pearl Harbor. The guide explained that the destroyer their glass-bottom boat was gliding over had flipped during the Japanese raid, trapping hundreds of men in air pockets when it sunk. The guide said that for one week rescuers could hear the trapped men tapping on the hull of the sunken boat. The guide said there was nothing anyone could do for them. Dave squinted into the Hawaiian sun and remembered the way the frog's front paws had worked the water.

3) Starlings. When he was duck hunting. He only went duck hunting the one time. All morning there were no ducks. Nothing in the water. Nothing in the sky. Just heavy grey clouds—just a smudge of sun at the end of the lake. Just before dawn a flurry of starlings flew overhead. Dave couldn't remember who was the first to shoot into the flock. He remembers lifting his borrowed rifle. Remembers the wonder he felt as the starlings tumbled out of sky. They hit the water like stones.

4) One groundhog. It was summer. He was a university student. He was working on a dairy farm in the Ottawa valley. He loved the job. He was driving tractors and cows. Every night after supper he took a .22-calibre rifle and walked through the fields. He watched the sun go down and smoked an Old Port cigarillo. He had the gun because he was supposed to shoot groundhogs. They dug tunnels in the fields. The tractor might tip into the tunnels. It made him feel important. The evening he saw his first groundhog she must have been a hundred yards away. She was sitting up in her hole like a prairie dog. The sun was behind him. He dropped to his knees and brought the rifle up to his shoulder. He squeezed the trigger. He was mortified when the groundhog dropped out of sight. She was lying on the ground when he walked up to her. There was a small red puncture in her side as if someone had driven a nail into her. Every time she breathed an awful sucking sound came out of the hole. Dave fumbled with the rifle. The bolt jammed. He couldn't get another bullet into the chamber. And the goddamn groundhog wouldn't die. Dave started to cry. "Die damn it," he yelled as he turned the rifle upside down and hit the groundhog with the butt. It was the last time he had ever shot a rifle.

5) One baby raccoon. Maybe two. It was night. He was driving his family back from a week's vacation by the ocean. They had just crossed the Appalachian

mountains. They were in a valley—on a two-lane highway. He was driving too fast. He saw the eyes glint in the darkness well ahead of him.

"Watch out," his wife said in the seat beside him. "I see it," he snapped, impatiently.

Saw with plenty of time to slow down. Instead he veered to the right. He still remembers the surprise, the shock when he heard the thump on his right bumper.

He had seen the flash of the mother's eyes in his headlights; what he hadn't seen were the babies who must have been following her across the highway. He had plowed right into them. He wanted to stop but his wife told him to keep going. The kids were in the back seat.

That's as far as Dave got on his list. It was after midnight. Everyone was asleep, except for the pig, who, not accustomed to having the lights on at this time of night, began to whistle from her cage on the counter. Dave got up and took a carrot out of the fridge and dropped it through the door on the top of the cage. The pig sniffed the carrot and settled down to it.

"Pig," said Dave out loud with great affection.

"Pig," he said again quietly to himself on his way up stairs to bed.

TUNNEL OF LOVE

At supper Stephanie said that she was thinking of becoming a witch. She said she had read about Wicca in *Mademoiselle* magazine. She said that ever since her cousin's wedding she *hated* Christianity—it was sooo...*chauvinistic*. She said Wicca wasn't like that.

As his daughter looked around the table, Dave dropped his attention to the food in front of him. He didn't want to look at his wife. He felt embarrassed that his daughter, their daughter, could say things like this. He felt responsible for this. He felt helpless.

"Good Brussels sprouts," he said. What he was trying to say was, This doesn't bother me. This is OK. What he wanted to say was, This scares me.

"They don't worship the devil or anything," said Stephanie. "White witches only cast good spells. You should read the article, Daddy. You could learn a lot."

Dave looked at his daughter across the table. She was wearing a black T-shirt and black jeans. Her complexion wasn't clear. She looked sullen. Unhappy. Angry. What have I done wrong? he thought. He felt sad and lost.

All he could think to say was, Excuse me.

"Excuse me," he said. He went upstairs.

"What's wrong with him?" asked Stephanie.

⊠ ⊠ ⊠

The next evening, when he got home from work, Dave pedalled his bike into the alley behind his house and confronted three indigent men propped against his neighbour's garage—their feet sticking into the alley.

The men leered up at him as he got off his bike. They were drunk. One of them had a bottle in a brown paper bag between his legs.

The men were wearing tank tops and Dave was close enough to see the menacing tattoos on their upper arms. The man closest to Dave was wearing a black civil war hat with a KISS badge sewn onto it. He had a goatee and an earring through his nose. It occurred to Dave that all three of the men looked surprisingly fit. That was when he noticed the three bikes. One was leaning against his garage door. Dave realized he was going to have to move the bike if he wanted to open his garage. He wondered whether he should leave it—go around to the front instead—and wheel his bike through the house and into the backyard. That way he wouldn't have to disturb them.

Instead he said, "I'm going to have move this bike to open my garage."

Dave was trying to be assertive. He was also trying to sound polite. There were, after all, three of them.

It was the man wearing the civil war cap who answered him. He was surprisingly contrite.

"I'm sorry," he said. "We just wanted to get away from the noise on Bloor Street." The man didn't make eye contact with Dave. He stared at the bottle between his legs while he was speaking.

"Don't break my bike," he added.

Dave moved the bike. Then he bent down to fiddle with the lock on his garage door. The three men stared sullenly at the ground. As he pulled the door open, Dave remembered an incident from the year he worked as a substitute teacher. He had gone for a walk at lunch time and inadvertently come across a group of students smoking at the far end of the football field. He remembered the five kids standing there defiantly with their cigarettes in their hands. Here he was, once again, ostensibly the guy with all the power. This was, after all, his house, his garage. Yet he was struck by the veneer of his authority. If these guys didn't want him to move their bikes what could he possibly do about it? They were the ones with the tattoos and the booze—he was the guy with the mortgage and the briefcase.

The lock clicked open and Dave wheeled his bike through the garage door. As he shut it behind him he heard the famous call of the Great White North ricochet through the alley.

Koo Roo Koo Koo
Koo Koo Koo Koo

It was the plaintive cry of Bob and Doug McKenzie from the SCTV television show. Dave was pretty sure it came from the guy with the civil war hat. But he didn't understand what he had meant by it. Whatever it was, his two friends thought it was pretty funny. Their raucous laughter was still echoing in his backyard as Dave walked inside his house.

No one was home.

Dave paced around the living room trying to figure out the joke.

He puzzled over it for fifteen minutes before the point of it descended upon him. He was the punch line.

Those bastards just called me a hoser, he said out loud.

He didn't know what to do with this information.

How do you demonstrate you're not a hoser to three drunks? If he went outside and tried to parade his non-hoserhood he would become, by definition, a hoser. He had no room to manoeuvre. He had been hosed—and without a single word spoken. Hosed with a sonorous cry from a drunk in an alley. His alley.

☒ ☒ ☒

"Stephanie wants to know if she can get her nose pierced," said his wife, Morley, after dinner. Dave was washing the dishes.

"What did you tell her. Does it leave a scar? What happens if you change your mind? Do you have a hole in your nose for the rest of your life?"

"No," said Stephanie, who, with uncanny timing,

walked into the kitchen. "It grows over. You just have a little black mark."

"A little black mark," repeated Morley.

"Scar," said Dave. "The word you're looking for is scar."

Dave went upstairs and lay on his bed and flipped through the newspaper. Why couldn't she just get pregnant or something straightforward? He finished the paper and thought, I am going to have to go downstairs eventually.

◼ ◼ ◼

When he woke up on Saturday the air in his bedroom was heavy and damp. He felt like he had wrestled the heat all night. The radio said the temperature was going to set an all-time high. The family dragged themselves through Saturday morning chores. When they finished, Dave said he would take everyone out to lunch before he went to the Record Store for the afternoon. We'll go some place with air-conditioning, he said. We'll cool off.

They went to Via Oliveto on Bloor Street. Dave had a beer and marinated calamari. He felt much better, but when he stepped out of the restaurant the heat hit him twice as hard as before he went in. Someone said the temperature was over one hundred. It felt like it.

As he crossed Bloor with his family, Dave held out his hand for Sam—his seven-year-old son. In his other hand he was carrying a bottle of apple juice which Sam hadn't finished. While they picked their way through the backed-up traffic, Dave spotted a Ford Fairlane trying to turn in front of them, from a side street, into the traffic. The driver looked aggravated. The car had been beautifully restored. It had a shiny black finish. It was in mint condition. Spotting an opening in the traffic the Fairlane jerked abruptly forward—so abruptly that its tires squealed. When he heard the noise, Dave realized that he and his family were in the car's way. He yanked Sam back but he didn't move himself and the black car almost knocked him over. Dave felt rage wash over him. Without thinking, he drew his hand back and launched the bottle of apple juice at the car. As soon as he let it go he thought: Oh my god what have I done? Then everything went into slow motion. The bottle spinning high in the air end over end and he thought, Jesus, it's going to go right over the car and hit the front windshield and cause an accident…the bottle arcing and tumbling through the air…it's going to hit the roof, maybe the back window. Sam is looking at his father with his mouth open, Morley looks horrified. The bottle descending now. The black car moving forward along Bloor.

Real time reasserted itself and the apple juice exploded on the back bumper.

Dave hustled his family into their car and pulled into the traffic. He soon realized that everyone had moved so fast that he had managed to pull out one car behind the Fairlane.

This is not a good idea, he thought. He turned left off Bloor onto Dalton Road.

As Dave drove north up Dalton he checked his rear-view mirror and saw that the Fairlane had made a U-turn and was following him up the street at great speed. Remembering the look on the guy's face, Dave turned to Morley and said, "I think that guy from Bloor Street is following us."

Morley has always disapproved of the aggressiveness that occasionally bubbles out of her husband when he gets behind the wheel of a car. They have fought about this. Mostly, Morley is afraid that Dave is going to yell at someone who is armed. She doesn't want her husband to be shot in an argument about driving manners. She has read about this happening somewhere.

Dave is now driving really quickly up Dalton. Sam is twisting to look out the back window, Morley is saying something, and Stephanie looks like she wants to be anywhere else but in this car, with this family. Dave is watching the Ford closing in in the rear-view mirror and watching the road up ahead which seems to be narrowing. Suddenly he sees construction workers, then the traffic stops and so does Dave. He sees the black Ford Fairlane pull up directly behind him.

"Lock the door," says Morley. "For God's sake don't get out, Dave. Dave?"

Dave's heart is pounding. He is dripping with sweat. He is thinking, If I stay in the car and he shoots me here someone else might get hurt. So he jumps out of the car to face the man from the black Ford, who has leapt out of his car and is coming towards him.

Dave is thinking, maybe I should hit him first. But before he is close enough to do anything he realizes the guy is actually apologizing.

He is saying, "I'm sorry. That was a really stupid thing I did. It was the heat. I was really uptight. Everyone is uptight. I thought I should apologize. Are you OK?"

Dave managed a meek apology of his own. "I shouldn't have thrown the bottle of juice," he said. They shook hands and got back in their cars and drove away.

"Oh, Canada," thought Dave.

⊠ ⊠ ⊠

That night Stephanie was invited to sleep over at a friend's house in Oakville.

"Will you drive her?" asked Morley.

It was about a fifty-minute drive each way. The Blue Jays were playing Boston. On the way home he could listen to baseball on the radio—he loved listening to baseball games on the radio—more than watching them on television—more even than going to the games. Maybe he would take the slow road by the lake. Maybe he'd take a beer and drink it while he drove.

They were about halfway to Oakville when Dave decided to say something that had been on his mind all week.

"I've been thinking about—about your nose," he said. That was as far as he could go. "...but I don't...I would have...I really think..."

He wanted to say he would rather have a needle in his eye than see his daughter with an earring in her nose.

"I decided not to get it pierced, Daddy. Jenny said it can get infected. It's really gross."

Dave felt a wave of euphoria wash over him.

He almost said, that's great. That's great.

Safe he thought. Safe at home. Free the bunch.

All he said was "Oh. Huh."

The Beatles came on the radio. "Eleanor Rigby." Neither of them said anything while the song was playing. The sun was starting to set and it was hard driving into the light. Dave reached for his sunglasses.

"Offspring are coming to the Gardens at the end of the month," said Stephanie. "Jenny and I want to go."

His daughter had never been to a rock concert before.

"The tickets go on sale next Saturday. Jenny is going to sleep over at the Gardens so we can get good seats. Can I go with her? Her mother doesn't want her to go alone."

Dave thought of the kids who came into his store and bought records by groups like Offspring. They all looked so much older than his daughter. He thought of Stephanie sharing a sleeping bag with some kid on Carlton Street. He felt a familiar wave of anxiety wash over him. It was like the time he had caught the kids smoking. He felt trapped in a position of power that he didn't want.

He shook his head. No, he said to himself.

Then he realized his daughter was saying something.

"Why not?" she said.

"Sorry?" said Dave.

"I knew you'd say no. You don't trust me."

"What?" said Dave. "I didn't mean you couldn't go. I meant…"

His daughter interrupted him. "Yes you did. You said no. I knew you'd say no. I told Jenny you'd say no."

Dave suddenly felt that no was what his daughter wanted him to say.

God help me, he thought. Here goes.

He said. "You're right I don't want you to go. I think fifteen is pretty young to be staying out all night."

Stephanie exhaled loudly.

"Fifteen is not young, Daddy."

She was staring straight ahead.

"Anyway. I'm almost sixteen."

Now what? he wondered. Now what happens? Now what do I say?

"You're right," he said. "Fifteen isn't young. Fifteen is old enough to decide these things. You can go if you want. But I'd rather you didn't."

That was true. That was what he thought.

Stephanie didn't say anything.

Neil Young came on the radio.

Stephanie said, "I hate this. Can I change the channel?"

"No," said Dave. "Yes. OK. Sure."

Stephanie reached out and twisted the dial. The music that filled the car was no longer the music of Dave's life. The rapid and repetitive base line perplexed him. It seemed to push him away.

Stephanie had her feet up on the dash, staring into the middle distance, mouthing words that Dave couldn't even make out.

She seemed so sure of herself.

He wondered if there had ever been a time in his life when he knew as much as she did.

Maybe his parents would say so.

He couldn't.

She said, "I don't really like Offspring anyway."

And then neither of them said anything for five minutes. They both concentrated on the road, on the cars around them.

Then Dave said, "Neither do I."

Stephanie laughed. Said, "You're not supposed to."

Two miles later she spotted a Dairy Queen. She said, "Can we get ice cream?"

Dave said, "Sure. Why not."

Ice cream would be great. The best.

Dave got a vanilla milkshake. Stephanie got a chocolate cone.

"Don't you want sprinkles?" he asked as he paid.

"Daddy," she said, shaking her head. Exasperated.

"Oh," he said. Dave was sure she had had sprinkles last time.

"Oh," he said again.

ROCK OF AGES

eorge Mills hadn't been well all winter but no one in Drumbolt expected him to die so abruptly. Especially Flora Perriton. Flora is one of Drumbolt's two music teachers. The other teacher is Muriel Hayes who, at seventy-six, is two years older than Flora.

Most people in Drumbolt assume that Flora and Muriel don't get along. It's easy to understand why they might think that. The two compete for what music business there is in town, and when you consider that there are only 578 people living there—577 now that George has gone—it doesn't leave a lot of slack in what you'd peg out as prime piano-lesson age. Drumbolt probably has more music teachers per capita than any town in the country. Because anyone with children must eventually choose one teacher over the other, some people feel uncomfortable if they happen to be talking to Flora outside the hardware store and they spot Muriel rounding the corner.

Flora and Muriel are always polite to each other, but there is no denying the awareness that hangs between them. Seeing them talking in the drugstore makes you think what it must be like when the chairman of the Ford Motor Company runs into the president of

General Motors at a fund-raiser.

Muriel teaches piano and violin. Flora teaches only piano. Some people say that Muriel's violin lessons appeal to the snobs in town; but the fact is Flora's students, year in and year out, win more awards at the Ayr Music Festival than Muriel's. Not that Flora keeps score. Or would mention it if she did. Except in a way that made it perfectly clear that it didn't matter to her one way or the other.

Flora teaches at the back of her house, and the kids let themselves in the side door by the wood stove without knocking.

Flora's late husband, Charlie, built the addition in the summer of 1975. That was the summer he retired. He had been talking about the addition for some time and Flora finally relented. She didn't give in because she thought they needed the space; they didn't. Their two boys had already moved out. She relented because she was afraid that Charlie was going to drive her crazy if he hung around the house with nothing to do. Charlie had worked at the Drumbolt Tent and Awning Company for thirty-four years. So she said, "You know that addition you've been talking about? I think it would be a good idea if we put it up this summer."

Charlie also came at the project with a hidden agenda. For years he had been trying to sell the addition to Flora as a room for her piano lessons. That way, he said, you won't have kids tracking through the house and messing up the parlour. But Charlie wasn't being completely honest because, in his heart of hearts, he saw the floor of Flora's new piano room as a roof for the basement he would have to dig and finish and panel. Charlie used to lie in bed at night and dream of the regulation-size-slate-bottom pool table you could put in such a basement. In fact he would lie in bed at night and imagine the games of pool he could play with his friend Frank Weir. He could almost hear the click of the balls as they danced across his regulation-size-slate-bottom table. Sometimes, after he had beaten Frank, Charlie would imagine conversations with him, and to his great pride he was always, in those late-night talks, generous to his friend and, modest too, about his talent in the great game of pool.

Charlie built the addition and got to play pool for about a year and a half before they found the tumour. He didn't play much in the seven months that it took him to die. You could count on your two hands the number of times that Flora has been in the pool room over the last eighteen years. But two years ago in September she decided she could not face another winter lugging firewood in from the shed every second day. So she had one of her students, Val Chambers, stack her wood neatly along the four walls of Charlie's pool room. Right on the carpet. That way every time she needed wood she could go downstairs and get it.

Although it made her life easier she wasn't happy with the arrangement. She knew that Charlie would spin in his grave if he could see what she had done and that bothered her. But when you are living alone, and the winter is cold, and you heat by wood, you do what you can do. But still, it bothered her. Sometimes in the afternoon before her classes began Flora would find herself staring into the downstairs bathroom mirror explaining to Charlie what it was like hauling wood from the shed every second day when you were seventy-four. But Charlie never understood. Charlie was still fifty-seven.

That was, in fact, what Flora was doing when the telephone rang. She was standing in the addition looking at the fireplace, feeling guilty about the wood downstairs. When she picked up the phone it was Eleanor Thacker calling to ask if she had heard about George Mills taking a stroke.

There are not many people left in Drumbolt who would remember that Flora Perriton was once sweet on George Mills. Eleanor, who was calling with the news, didn't know. And when she told Flora, she couldn't see her standing there in the hall with her hand up to her mouth, not moving. After they said goodbye Flora went back to the bathroom and looked in the mirror and uttered the ultimate insult. She looked at herself and said with great sadness, "Oh, you old woman." She said it twice. "Oh, you old woman."

George Mills had phoned her only last fall, and asked if he could take her out for supper. She hadn't gone. She had wanted to go. But for some reason she didn't understand she told George that she was busy. She hated herself for doing that. She remembered the night when she was a young school teacher and George Mills had come to her house for supper and they had sat on the couch and he had kissed her and they had lain there and held each other tight on the floor by the fireplace. She had thought of that night a lot and wondered if it would have been so terribly wrong for George Mills to come to her house again so she could cook dinner and they could sit in the new addition by the wood stove. Would it have been so wrong if he had held her again? If he had put his arms around her and hugged her? It had been almost twenty years since a man had held her.

Of course as soon as she got thinking like that she would go to the bathroom and apologize to Charlie. But what could she do? Charlie never understood. She knew he would be apoplectic if he were to walk in and find her hugging George Mills in the addition that he had built just before he died. When she thought about it, she decided he would probably be more upset if he went downstairs to his pool room and found the two cords of wood stacked on the carpet. She never phoned George back. The last time she had seen him was at the Ayr Fair. Now they were going to bury him, and her last chance for a hug, on Friday.

She went to the service alone. She walked to the church after lunch. It was a simple service. There was no choir and no solo planned. Flora doesn't sing solo in public any more. She doesn't like the sound of an old woman's voice. Especially hers. She says she can't stand the way her voice wavers on the high notes, and the way you can hear her gasping for breath. She says she sounds like a dying fish. She said it enough that Reverend Godkin gave up asking her to sing five years ago, and since there is no one else he can ask, if you are getting married, or buried, in Drumbolt these days you have to be happy with the musical talents of the congregation.

But when Jeannette Bailey started up the organ for the closing hymn, "Rock of Ages," Flora broke out of the gate ahead of the pack. She started singing a half a beat in front of everyone else. When she did that, the entire congregation pulled up short. For the briefest moment everyone in the church froze with their mouths open and their chests full. Were they supposed to be singing or not? They were all counting on giving George an almighty choral farewell but no one wanted to make the first move. No one wanted to look foolish. So they checked themselves for a beat to see if anyone else joined in. Of course no one did and by that time Flora had sung the first line right to the end and what was supposed to be a rousing hymn was quickly becoming a solo. Flora didn't notice she was singing alone until she got to the end of the second line and she couldn't very well stop there, so she kept going. You can imagine how uncomfortable everyone felt standing up and not singing, so when Reverend Godkin nodded, Frank Weir sat down and with great relief everyone else joined him. That left Flora all alone. Singing. Beautifully.

> While I draw this fleeting breath,
> When my eyes shall close in death,
> When I rise to worlds unknown,
> And behold Thee on Thy throne,
> Rock of Ages, cleft for me,
> Let me hide myself in Thee.

Not a person in the room noticed that her breath wasn't what it used to be, or that she wavered on the high notes. Eleanor said George would have cried if he could have heard it. Frank Weir was so moved that he nearly applauded, but he remembered where he was and stopped himself in time. As for Flora, it may not have been as good as a hug, but it was the best she could do.

After the service Reverend Godkin told her it was nice to have her sing like that and asked if she would do it again some Sunday. Flora said that she would think about it and, no, she didn't mind him asking, and she had always liked George Mills, but she had to run. She had Andy McLeod at four o'clock.

THE JOCK STRAP

utumn was moving faster than Morley liked. The kids had settled in school and though it wasn't yet November you wouldn't know it for the rain. Morley had spent July and the better part of August at the lake with her in-laws. She knew her friends, most of whom spent their summers lugging kids back and forth to the park, envied her those two months. Everyone said she was lucky to have Willa and Bud. Morley didn't try to explain the sense of doom she felt each June as her car lurched over the gravel hill and onto the lake road. She knew she shouldn't complain about her in-laws. But she had been going to their cottage every summer for ten years, and she imagined Julys and Augusts weren't much different for her than they were for Terry Anderson when he was held hostage in Beirut. What could make you more heavy hearted, she wondered, than to sit beside your mother-in-law while she mended your children's clothes. Morley felt each poke of the needle as if it was going into her back.

When she came back to the city, Morley promised herself that she wouldn't go to the lake again.

On the Sunday night before the kids started school she sat at the kitchen table with a cup of coffee and wrote out a schedule for the year she was facing. She taped it inside the cupboard door where she kept the breakfast cereals so she would see it every morning. Monday: Wash bedclothes and towels, garbage, water plants, vacuum. Tuesday: Clean out micro-wave, pay bills, fix things.

She set aside Sunday nights for sewing. If she stuck to it she'd get through the pile in no time. She mended three out of the first four weeks and thought she was doing well until, at the beginning of October, she realized that instead of shrinking, the pile was growing. She was adding things to it that she would not have considered repairing before. None of them hers. She hemmed her dresses with masking tape. She used safety pins for missing buttons. "If God had wanted me to sew," she had once said to Dave, as she repaired a hole in one of his pockets, "why would he have given me this." She was holding a stapler at the time.

Morley knew she was licked the Tuesday morning she brought the blue corduroys downstairs for Stephanie. It had taken all evening to put patches on both knees. It had never occurred to her that Steph might have outgrown them. She knew when to quit. At lunch she went upstairs and sorted through the sewing pile. Most of it she put back in the drawers. The rest she threw out. She wasn't particularly proud. But she felt better. She drove to McDonald's and had a hamburger and a cup of coffee and read the paper. Her list said she should be fixing things. In a way she was.

⊠　⊠　⊠

Saturday was Sam's first day at hockey. The notice said he had to wear complete equipment. Morley had been accumulating things for a year. On Wednesday night she laid them out on the kitchen table. The blue pants looked too large for her son. She had rescued them from her nephew Scott. One of the thigh pads was missing but she thought she could cut one out of cardboard. She looked at her list and ticked off pants. The skates, she figured, would hold up another year. She ticked off skates. Then she ticked off elbow pads. She had bought them from the lady across the street. The shin guards came from a church sale. The kids had worn them on their shoulders for two years now for dress-up. Sally said she thought she had a helmet that would fit Sam and had promised to bring it to the rink. Morley ticked off shin guards and put a question mark beside helmet. She stuffed everything into two plastic bags, propped them by the door and went upstairs.

This is a father's job, she thought to herself as they drove to the rink the next morning. Bruce had phoned in sick and Dave had gone to open the store. Sam was alone in the back seat holding his stick. They weren't talking. They had a fight after breakfast because Sam wanted to get dressed at home. The only thing he had said in the last thirty minutes was that they were going to be late. The second time he said it Morley told him to *get into the car.* Now she was regretting yelling. Why did they have to fight before his first game of hockey? Is this what he would remember?

In the dressing room Sam slumped on the bench and Morley stared at the two bags. For the first time in her life she had no idea how to dress her son. She didn't know where to begin. The man beside her was lacing his boy into a set of shoulder pads. She didn't have shoulder pads. The list said they were optional.

"We don't have those," Sam said, accusingly.

"We don't have to," Morley said. "You don't have to have them."

She started with the pants.

Then she was stumped.

"Do the shin pads," said the man beside her. "then put the socks over."

Sam was the last kid on the ice.

◼ ◼ ◼

On Thursday after school Sam said he needed a jock strap.

"What for?" said Morley. She was frying sausages for dinner and reading a gardening magazine.

"Everyone has one. I have to."

"WHO has one?" she said.

"Paul. He wore it to school. It's a penis protector."
Morley phoned Paul's mother after supper.

❑ ❑ ❑

Friday morning Morley drove to Canadian Tire. When
she got there she sat in the parking lot. She wasn't sure
what to ask for. She knew penis protector couldn't be
right but she wasn't sure about jock strap. She didn't
know if it was a word you could use in a Canadian Tire
store. It might be a little-boy word. Like fart. She certainly wasn't about to say penis to a man she didn't know.

She drove home and phoned Dave.

"Sam needs a jock strap for hockey," she said.
"That's your job."

"OK," he said, without enthusiasm.

Great, she thought.

❑ ❑ ❑

Saturday Morley took Steph to get her hair cut. Dave
took Sam to hockey.

"How was the jock?" Morley asked at supper.

"It didn't fit," said Sam, pointing at his father as if
he was a witness in a murder trial. "He didn't get the
holder."

◪ ◧ ◪

Morley opened her son's equipment bag on Wednesday night and fished out the jock strap. It looked just like the masks painters wear on their faces when they are sanding dry wall. It was a size—medium.

She phoned Paul's mother again.

"That's just the cup," Maggie explained. "There's a holder it slips into. Like a garter belt."

How could Dave watch all the hockey he watched and not get the holder? The way he hollered during hockey games you would think he had at least a rudimentary knowledge of the equipment. How could he sit in front of the television so full of opinions and come home with a cup and no cup holder? Morley felt resentment well up in her as she thought of the Saturday nights she had struggled to get the kids into bed while Dave sank into the couch in front of a hockey game. If he hadn't *learned* anything, what was the point?

◪ ◧ ◪

Morley went back to Canadian Tire on Thursday night. As she passed through the automatic doors she realized she still didn't know what the holder was called. She had looked over the equipment list again before she had

left home. Jock strap definitely wasn't on it. She had a
tick beside everything on the list except shoulder pads.
She had double checked. Shoulder pads *were* optional.

There were four aisles of hockey equipment. She
spotted the holder on her second pass. They came in
three sizes: medium, large and extra large. All things
considered she was surprised to see how small the extra
large one was. The package came with a cup identical
to the one Dave had bought plus the elastic belt he had
neglected. Morley was holding a medium in her hand
when she saw the salesman coming. This was what she
was hoping to avoid.

"For your husband?" he asked.

"My son," said Morley.

"How old is he?"

Thank God, thought Morley. She thought he was
going to ask how big it was.

"He's seven," she said. All she could think about was
Sam's tiny penis—stuck in the space between his legs
like the snout of a baby anteater.

"This is too big," said the young man taking the
package from her. "You'll need extra extra small...we're
out. Try maybe Eaton's."

She was smiling when she got back to the car.
Athletic Support it had said in big white letters on the
red package. It was on her list after all. She had ticked it
off. Morley thought *she* was the Athletic Support.

She got the jock at the Bay. "An extra-extra-small athletic support for a seven-year-old boy. He is playing

hockey," she said nonchalantly. "It's his second year." She wasn't sure why she added the lie.

Sam put it on as soon as she got home. He put it on over his pants. Then before she could stop him he ran across the street to show Allen. Why not? thought Morley. She watched them from the window. Sam standing proudly on the front lawn. He looks like a ballet dancer, she thought. Then Allen kicking him between the legs. Her son laughing. He wore the jock to bed that night. And to school the next day, under his jeans. Morley was going to say no, and then she thought, Why not? For a week she kept finding it all over the house—on the stairs, on the couch in the TV room, slung over his chair in the kitchen. She felt no compulsion to put it away. She was as pleased with it as he was.

NEW YORK CITY

At first Ed thought it was just luck, turning on the radio and hearing three Big Al Brown tunes in a row. Then he wondered, maybe Big Al is coming to town. Felt a tickle of anticipation and thought, No, I would have heard about that. Doesn't notice, until he is pulling into the parking lot, that the DJ is using the past tense. Then sits there for five minutes hardly moving. Al Brown? Dead?

The parking lot attendant comes over and asks if he is OK.

"What?" says Ed. "Oh. Just listening to the radio."

Doesn't get out of the car. Doesn't even get the engine turned off. Turns around and drives out of the lot. Waves sheepishly at the attendant. Goes home.

After supper Ed sits at the kitchen table listening to his Al Brown records, letting the pedal steel guitar and the thin harmonies carry him away. Just drunk enough to pick up the broom as he glides over to the fridge, singing into the handle as he goes, getting most of the words right.

Until Carol shouts downstairs to *turn the music down.*

"Sorry," says Ed, to himself, turning it down but

probably not enough for Carol. Calls back, "I can't believe he's dead."

Carol doesn't hear.

"Who cares?" says Ed.

On Saturday morning when he wakes up he wakes up thinking about Al Brown. It's like the morning after his mother died—sad before he gets his eyes open.

Anna was eighty years old when she died. Lived the last two years of her life at the Wildwood Seniors' Residence. A room on the third floor. Nice coral walls, is what the woman who showed Ed around said. They won't glare in the afternoon. Won't hurt her eyes.

Anna. Anna. Born in Hungary in 1915. Made it to Montreal in 1935. Young enough and pretty enough and with just enough English to land a job at the *Montreal Standard*. Payroll Department. Was shown around the city by a young reporter named Mavis Young. Mavis took her to parties. Once she met Dr. Norman Bethune. It was the same night she met Frank. "I could have gone with the doctor," she used to say, when she was feeling especially affectionate towards her husband. "I could have."

She loved the Plouffe family. And Juliette. Hated Wayne and Shuster. Read Gabrielle Roy, Roger Lemelin and poems by Frank Scott. Became a fan of hockey. Maurice Richard. The great Jean Beliveau.

After Frank died, and everyone else had given up on hockey, Anna still watched the games every Saturday night. When she was seventy-five years old she was the

only person Ed knew who could name all twenty-one
teams in the National Hockey League. The summer
before she died she stopped speaking English. She
would only speak Hungarian. It seemed out of her control. As if Hungary was reaching out. Reclaiming her.

For a while Ed visited Anna three, four times a week.
He was attracted to the nurse who did nights on the
third and fourth floors. Sat by her desk and talked
while Anna watched television. The nurse's name was
Carol. Every time he said her name Ed had to concentrate not to call her Cheryl by mistake. His ex-wife was
Cheryl. This was Carol.

One Saturday morning Ed asked Carol if she would
help him take Anna for a drive. She said sure. Carol was
going off duty but she wore her uniform and told herself she was still working.

They went to the Elora Gorge. Had lunch in a little
tea house with six tables. They dropped Anna at the
Wildwood just before supper. Ed said, "Carol, I'll drive
you home?" When they were in front of her apartment
Carol said, "Do you want to come in for a coffee or
something?" They talked for hours before Ed got up the
nerve to reach out and pat her in—what was it?
Reassurance? Let his hand linger along her creamy arm,
and when he saw her fingers twitch, he took a chance.
Reached up and touched her face. Carol smiled at him.
Yes? Ten minutes later they were making love on the
sofa. Ed still in his socks, his pants strangling his

ankles. His eyes squeezed shut. He looked like a snake shedding its skin. They were married six months later.

Carol wore cardigans and plaid skirts. She fixed her hair the way Mary Tyler Moore did when she played that TV reporter. Actually cut a picture out of a magazine and took it to her hairdresser. Said, like this, sort of. She hardly ever used make-up, though sometimes, when they were going out, she put on lipstick. But always, much to Ed's relief, she would sit in the car, peering in the rear-view mirror, dabbing at her lips with Kleenex, until the lipstick hardly showed.

She kept working at the Wildwood but they never told Anna. Never told her that Cheryl had left Ed. Never told her that he and Carol were married. It would have only upset her. What was the point?

⊠ ⊠ ⊠

Ed had seen Big Al three times in his life. Once on his honeymoon—the first one—with Cheryl. They were driving through New England in his wood-panelled Vega wagon. The clutch dropped out near the border and they rolled into a small-town garage making a racket you could hear for blocks. It was Friday night—they were closing—but the guy in the garage drove to the Auto-Mart and got the part they needed. Ed helped fix the clutch. All greasy. Swearing and grunting. Cheryl sitting on a bridge chair watching them work. Disgusted by the crack that appeared at the top of the mechanic's bum every time he bent over. At nine she left the garage and went to the movies. Saw Sean Connery in *Diamonds Are Forever*. When she came back the clutch was finished and Ed and the guy from the garage were drinking beer.

"A hundred and sixty-eight dollars. You know what that would have cost in Toronto?" said Ed as they pulled out of town.

They drove until two in the morning. Trying to make up time. Until Cheryl said, "We've got to stop." She watched from the front seat, so tired it seemed like a dream, Ed banging on the door of the Ethan Allen Motel.

It was the next day at lunch when Ed heard the ad for the Al Brown concert. He heard it on the radio in a diner where they were eating fried clams.

"I've wanted to see Al Brown all my life," he said. Excited. Thinking to himself, what makes this so great is having Cheryl to share it with. Unbelievable.

Cheryl thinking, He's more excited about the god-damn concert than this honeymoon.

They drove to Portland and Ed got a pair of tickets from a kid on the street. Even Cheryl had to admit it was a good show.

Next time maybe five years later. Ed drove to Buffalo to see him. Cheryl couldn't go. She was in her last year of architecture school at the University of Toronto. Working on a big project. Didn't want to see Al Brown again.

The show was even better than Portland. Al Brown pinned to the stage by a razor-sharp blue spotlight. The back-up singers, lit in orange, swaying behind him. There was steam and smoke swirling in the lights.

It was during this concert that Ed realized that no other music touched him like Al Brown's songs. He felt sheepish about this. He knew the music wasn't sophisticated or even soulful. Cheryl used to sneer at it. Even Carol teased him about it. He had learned not to go around telling people he liked Al Brown. But at the concert he realized if they were going to release a soundtrack of *his* life the tunes would all be by Al Brown. Al Brown said things for him. Some of the songs, like, "Never Alone, Always Apart" or "I'll Call You Next Time I'm in Town" seemed to have been written just for Ed. What surprised him was that this was apparently true for others too.

When he walked into the Buffalo Auditorium he felt queerly uncomfortable. There were so many other... fans. He felt...jealous? Exposed? Shy? What did he expect? To be all alone? Halfway through the concert he stood up and began dancing like everyone else. He was in Buffalo for God's sake. Who was going to recognize him?

After the show he got a motel room in Niagara Falls—American side. He went shopping the next morning. Got a pair of Lee jeans with a button fly and a striped shirt from a factory outlet. He tore off the tickets and wore the jeans and the shirt over the border. Said, "No," when the woman at customs asked if he had anything to declare.

Cheryl had spent the weekend planning a low-income housing development. The kitchen table was covered with drawings. The sink was full of dishes. She wanted to show Ed everything she had done. She didn't even ask about the concert.

One evening, two months later, while they were cleaning up after supper, Ed washing the dishes, Cheryl said, "I want a divorce." Right out of the blue. Not, I'm unhappy. Not, Ed, I want to have children. The funny thing was, Ed thought they had a good marriage. He didn't know what to say. It was a Wednesday night. She moved out on the weekend.

Al Brown had himself been divorced twice. Three times if you counted the year and a half he toured with Roseanne Cash.

Ed couldn't believe he was dead. Christ, he said out loud on Saturday afternoon, dropping underwear into the washer, humming the tune he had played over and over when Cheryl left.

What's the use of loving you
If you're not loving me.

Carol was at the library with the kids.

Al was buried on Nantucket Island. Ed bought *People* magazine so he could read about the funeral. Roseanne Cash and Dolly Parton sang by the grave—an a cappella version of "Stand By Your Man." Ed stared at the picture of Big Al's wife, his little girl.

When he was seven Ed saw Gene Autry, the singing cowboy, at the Montreal Forum. He could remember him riding around the ring. Singing. But he couldn't remember the rest of the show. Was it a rodeo? That year he got a red cowboy guitar with a white lariat painted around the music box.

He never learned how to finger a chord but he remembered putting on shows for his parents. Bouncing on his bed in his polo pyjamas.

Besides Gene Autry he loved show tunes. *My Fair Lady*, *South Pacific* and *Oklahoma*. When he was alone in the house he would put the records on. Then he would sing along, jumping around the room. Show records were the only music that Frank and Anna bought. They would go to a play at Her Majesty's Theatre on Guy Street and bring back a soundtrack album the way other people might bring home a program. He couldn't remember them playing the records. He was the one who played the music.

He bought his first record, a 78 r.p.m., when he was seven. "Twenty-six Miles Across the Sea." The Four Preps.

When he was eight he went into the local record store by himself for the first time. Anna waited outside in the car. It wasn't a record store exactly. It was a radio repair shop that sold records. He asked for the song that he thought was called "A Mawsha Cup." The

owner, a large man in an open-necked shirt and cardi-
gan, peered at him dimly as he shoved his dollar up and
over the tall counter.

"A Mawsha Cup," he repeated.

"Hey, Steve," called the fat owner to his assistant in
the back, his piggy eyes lighting up in sudden recogni-
tion. "Come here."

Turning to Ed, "Tell Steve what you want."

They were laughing at him.

He carried the record outside. A heavy black lacquer
orb. Anna waiting in the car. He had been humiliated.
Felt as brittle as the disc. The name of the tune was
"I'm All Shook Up."

One year for his birthday he got a red leather book that
looked like a photo album. It had sleeves made of thick
brown paper. It was designed to store his 45 r.p.m.
records. There was an index at the beginning and Ed
numbered each page and carefully wrote the names of
his records in the index with a fountain pen. He used
Peacock-blue ink. He got a thick metal cylinder like the
cardboard tube inside a roll of toilet paper so he could
stack the records on the record player and they would
drop down one after the other.

When he was sixteen he lost all these records at a
party. Somebody stole them. It had to be someone he
knew. He looked everywhere. Asked everyone. No one
owned up. Years later he came to think of the theft as
just. He himself had stolen many of the records in his
collection. Not from other kids but from a place on

Sherbrooke Street. It was an all-purpose store that sold groceries and paperback books and magazines and had a soda counter and a few booths. He would slip the records into his school bag. He was never caught.

He stole seven the Friday night that John Kennedy was shot. Anna made him turn off the television and come downstairs to eat supper. He wanted to watch TV. He stormed out of the house slamming the door, yelling. He went to the restaurant and watched the television behind the counter. He ate French-fried potatoes for supper.

When he was in college he was caught leaving the Miracle Mart with the Beatles' "Abbey Road" album tucked under his arm. They took his name and two months later he was summoned to a lawyer's office. They told him they would press charges if they ever caught him stealing again. He never did.

At the end of May *People* magazine ran a picture of Al Brown's widow on the cover. They called the article "Love Left Behind." It was the title of Al's biggest hit. Inside there was a picture of Al's daughter standing with her mother in front of their New York City apartment. The caption under the picture said the girl was eleven. Ed thought she could be fifteen. He saved the magazine. He began to have conversations with Al's widow as he walked to work. He imagined himself as her confidant. They talked about whether to bring out another record—there were over twenty Al Brown songs that had been recorded and never released. Some days he said they should go ahead with the record. It would be like a tribute. They could call it "Al Brown— Encore." Or maybe, "After the Show." Other days he thought they should leave it.

"If he had wanted those songs brought out he would have done it," he said one day as he crossed Dundas Street, on his way into the Eaton Centre to eat lunch at the Food Court.

There was a grocery store in the background of one of the pictures in *People*. It occurred to Ed if he could find the grocery store he could find the apartment where Al had lived. He phoned information in New York City. There were four stores with the same name. He had to phone twice to get all four phone numbers. It wouldn't be hard to find the addresses. He could phone the stores for free from work.

Ed had met Al Brown once. It was that time in Maine with Cheryl. It was Cheryl who had pointed him out. They had arrived in Portland early enough to have dinner before the show. The tour bus was parked on the same street where they had left their car. Cheryl said, "There's Al Brown." Ed said, "He has more hair than that." Was about to say, "That guy is too old," when someone asked the guy for an autograph and then people were taking his picture and Cheryl wanted Ed to get out of the car so she could take his picture with Al Brown but he didn't let her. Said he didn't want to bother Al. Stood on the edge of the crowd and watched. Stepped forward as Al was about to climb onto his bus and held out his hand stiffly and said, "Your songs have given me a great deal of pleasure." Al said, "Thanks." And got on the bus. Now Ed wished he had let Cheryl take the picture.

He didn't know what to make of it—the way he was feeling. He had never felt like this about a public figure before. He hadn't been this upset when Anna had died. But Anna was old. Anna was supposed to die.

Kept thinking that Al had made it through so much. Two divorces. Heroin. Alcohol. The motorcycle accident. He had been living with the same woman for what? Ten, twelve years now. It was all in the music. The pain, the years alone. The triumph of L-O-V-E.

That was the name of his last album. Christ. It *was* the last album.

Ed felt like he had lost a friend.

Earlier that year Ed's friend Don had a tumour removed from his lungs. Ed visited him in the hospital after the operation. Embarrassed at first—like they shouldn't talk about it or something. Now Al Brown has a heart attack and dies. What was going on?

He phoned a travel agent and booked a flight to New York City. He told Carol he was going up north for the weekend—to work on the cottage. He did this every spring. One weekend alone. Was she sure she didn't mind? Didn't want to come? I'll be back on Sunday, he said. After supper.

⊠ ⊠ ⊠

Ed has never been in New York City before. When the taxi driver at La Guardia asks him where he wants to go he says the only place he knows. The Empire State Building. Tries to say it as if he goes there all the time. Doesn't want the driver to rip him off.

He is jumpy. Terrified. He feels like he is cheating on Carol. Afraid he will run into someone who knows them. What could he say?

In his pocket he has a piece of paper with four addresses written on it. He hasn't the faintest idea where any of them are. He is not one of those people born with an innate understanding of New York City. The East Side. The West Side. The Village. The east side of what? He feels like he has fallen out of a boat into the middle of the ocean. He keeps bumping into things.

He finds the grocery store just before noon on Saturday. There is a luncheonette at the end of the street. He buys a coffee and a chocolate doughnut and takes them to a table by the window. The doughnut is stale. He feels anxious. He is in a coffee shop in New York City watching the apartment where he thinks Al Brown used to live—where he thinks his widow lives today. He has no idea what he is going to do if the woman he is waiting for comes outside.

He sees them at four o'clock. Robin, her name is Robin. Shoulder-length red hair. Red lipstick. She is wearing jeans and a white shirt that was made for a man. Big Al? The shirt isn't tucked in. She is holding her daughter's hand. Big Al's daughter. Her name is Allison. Robin is holding a violin case. She must be taking Allison to a music lesson.

Ed is still sitting in the luncheonette. He calls the waitress over.

"How much," he says. "How much do I owe you?"

The waitress wants to write out a bill.

Ed doesn't have time for this.

"What about ten dollars?" he says. "Will ten dollars do?"

He pushes a twenty-dollar bill into the waitress's hand and runs out the door.

He catches up to Robin and Allison at the corner of 71st and Riverside. They are waiting for a street light to change. He is standing right behind them. If he wanted, he could lean forward and smell Robin's hair. He imagines the three of them back in the apartment together. He has thought about this. They are eating spaghetti, playing Monopoly, laughing. Wonders if they have laughed since Al died. He can feel his eyes filling with tears. Christ, he is crying. He wants to stop them. All he wants to say is, I'm sorry.

The light changes and Robin and Allison cross to the far corner. Ed doesn't. He follows them from the other side of the street. It is a trick that he has learned from spy novels.

The mother and daughter go into a Korean grocery store. Ed waits where he is. They seem to be taking forever. He hears a siren. It is coming naggingly closer. Have they spotted him? Did they call the police? Maybe this happens all the time. There is another siren now, coming from a different direction. Ed's heart accelerates. He should leave but he doesn't know which way to go. He turns and heads back towards the luncheonette. A police car sweeps past him and keeps going. He looks back. The mother and her little girl are coming out of the store. The girl is eating a candy bar. The mother is carrying a plastic bag. It looks heavy.

Ed is following them again. They turn into a lavish yellow-stone building that occupies the entire block between 73rd and 74th. It is festooned with lacy iron balconies. Perhaps this is where the girl has her music lesson.

Ed crosses the street and walks past the main floor arcade. "The Ansonia" reads the sign set into the stone. The building feels strangely familiar. He has the peculiar sensation of having been here before. He checks his watch. How long could a music lesson last? Half an hour? Forty-five minutes?

At five past five the girl and her mother reappear. Robin is still carrying the plastic bag. The girl is carrying the violin case.

Why hadn't he written a letter? If he had written a letter he could have handed it to them and walked away. He could have put his address on it so they could have written him if they wanted. Why hadn't they gone somewhere else? Like the zoo. They must go to the zoo sometimes. If they had gone to the zoo it would have been easy for him to strike up a conversation. Something about the animals. *Look at that. I'm from Toronto. Only get down here every few months. There's a train in the Toronto zoo. You ride in the train and the animals are free to walk around these big compounds. Give me your address and I'll send you a postcard of the pandas from China.* After a few months he could have written that he was coming again and asked if they would like to meet him at the zoo for...for what? Lunch. For lunch. That would be normal enough. That wouldn't be crazy. He certainly couldn't go up to them and say I'm from Canada. I've been following you. That was crazy. He could get arrested.

While they were waiting for the light at the corner of West End and 74th, Ed crosses so he is standing behind them again. It is only half a block to their apartment. This could be his last chance. He couldn't come this far and not say anything.

"Excuse me," he says. .

Allison turns and looks up at him.

And in that split second, when the girl's eyes meet his, the hundreds of things that Ed has imagined saying desert him—all his fantasies vanish—like a flock of crows lifting off a bare-limbed tree. Leaving Ed staring at the girl, with nothing coming out his mouth.

"Mummy?" says Allison.

Robin stops.

She turns and sees Ed. And Ed sees fear wash across her face. This isn't what he planned. This isn't what he wanted at all. He feels trapped.

He feels like he is standing on the street with nothing on.

"Excuse me," he hears himself say. He is tugging at his sweater, pulling it down to cover his wrist. "Do you have...the time?"

It was the only thing he could think of.

"Oh," says Robin. "I'm sorry. It's...."

She had already begun moving down the street again. Stopping now. Turning. Checking her watch. Smiling. Her red hair.

"It's twenty past five."

And now Ed is thinking, I am Babe Ruth. The ball is hanging over the plate as full as the moon. If I don't swing right now, I don't get another chance.

And in that timeless moment he forgets that he is married. Has children. Works in the Personnel Department at Ontario Hydro. Forgets he coaches his daughter in Little League baseball on Saturday mornings. Forgets Big Al Brown. Forgets why he has come to New York City.

He remembers instead a spring afternoon when he was six years old. Anna has taken him on the bus to the stores in Westmount. She is going to buy him a new pair of shoes. There is an X-ray machine in the shoe store. You can stick your feet into a slot at the bottom of the machine and look through the top and see your feet right through your shoes—the bones and everything. Ed spends fifteen minutes watching his toes wiggling in the phosphorescent green light.

The shoes they buy are brown and made of leather. He is wearing them as they walk home along Sherbrooke Street, looking down at his feet every few minutes. Anna is carrying his old shoes in a brown paper bag. It is nearly supper. He is hungry. They stop and buy a half-dozen bagels. They eat one each as they walk along the street. It is wonderful to walk with your mother like this.

The man who is walking towards them looks at their bagels and says something that Ed doesn't hear. Did he say something was dirty? No, he couldn't have said dirty because Anna is saying, thank you. Thank you, Sir. That is a compliment. She has stopped walking. She is standing in the middle of the sidewalk watching the man walk away. Ed feels embarrassed.

What did he say? What did he say?

He said... He said we were Jews.

Why did you say thank you?

Because it is a nice thing to say to a person. It is a compliment. To be a Jew.

Ed is aware again of the woman standing in front of him on the New York street. Aware of the woman but not of the city. He doesn't hear the sirens, the cars, the hum. All this has faded. There is, for this moment, just Ed, this woman and her child. It is true, as Babe Ruth used to say, you *can* see the stitches in the ball as it tumbles towards the plate. Ed feels as if he has all the time in the world. Time to consider every possible thing he might say. Time to evaluate the consequences of saying it. It is, as they say, as if the world has stopped spinning.

He had asked them the time. They had told him.

"Thank you," he says.

And he smiles and walks past them. Past their apartment with the doorman waiting for them to sweep in. Happy. Safe. Together. A mother and her daughter home from a violin lesson late on a Saturday afternoon. And Ed too, happy, as he walks through this New York evening, whistling on his way to the hotel he is staying at on Broadway. That was an Al Brown tune. *A Hotel on Broadway.* Whistling again later that night as he walks to Times Square and buys a discounted ticket for a musical he has read about.

BREAKFAST, LUNCH, DINNER

n Saturday morning at 5:45 Dave gasped and sat up with a start. He could feel his heart thumping against his chest. My God, he thought, I'm having a heart attack.

"Morley," he said to his wife, trying to remember what you were supposed to do when The Big One hit.

Then he heard the voice.

There was someone else in the bedroom with them.

He didn't recognize the voice.

Had he passed out? Was it the ambulance driver?

Dave felt like he was swimming underwater, struggling to get to the surface, struggling to assemble himself, pull himself together...to Wake Up.

He hadn't passed out.

They were being robbed.

What a time to have a heart attack.

"Morley?" he said again.

He was still asleep.

At some level he understood this.

But his heart was still racing.

The voice was still there.

It was saying something about...an all-day sale at a car dealership?

Why would a burglar be telling him this?

"Shit, Dave."

Morley poked her husband in the back.

"The radio, Dave."

Dave had moved the clock radio off his bedside table and onto the bureau. He had moved it because of something he had read about electro-magnetic emissions and brain tumours.

"I don't know," he said when Morley asked. "Better to be safe than sorry, I guess."

Morley hadn't said anything but he knew she didn't approve.

He stumbled to the bureau and dopey with sleep managed to turn the volume up rather than off.

Morley swore again and disappeared under a pillow.

Dave slapped frantically at the radio and the alarm began barking. It was his turn to swear. He reached down and pulled the plug out of the wall.

"There," he said.

It was still dark. Dave was standing in the middle of the room holding the plug as if he had just landed the first fish of the year. He knew he wasn't about to fall back to sleep.

"Shit," he said again, and went downstairs to fetch the paper.

On Sunday Dave and Morley slept in.

Monday too.

Dave forgot he had unplugged the alarm.

He didn't wake up until Sam tried to climb into bed with him. It was five past eight.

STUART MᶜLEAN

"Shit," he said for the third time since Saturday.

By the time he got downstairs everything was moving too fast for anyone's good. Sam was pouring his own cereal, getting most of it into the bowl. Morley was peeling a carrot into the sink, too focused to notice Sam's mess. Holding the carrot out like she was doing a cooking demonstration.

"Who's celery?" she asked. "Who's carrots?"

Why could she never remember this?

"Me," said Stephanie her mouth full of toast.

"Me, what?" said Morley. "Me carrots? Or me celery?"

It was 8:40. Both kids should have left for school.

"You should eat something," said Dave to his wife as he ducked around Sam on his way to the sink. Knowing, even as the words left his mouth, that this wasn't helpful. What he wanted to say was, "I feel guilty eating when you are running around."

What his wife heard was, "It's your fault we are late."

"I need a prescription slip," said Sam, as his father tied his shoes. "We're going on a field trip. To Humpty Dumpty."

"You are going where?" asked Dave, incredulous.

"He needs a note," said Morley from the kitchen.

"To go to a potato chip factory? This is a school trip? You're going to a potato chip factory?"

"I need a note or I can't go."

"Where's the letter from school? I want to see this," said Dave.

"I don't know. I think it's in my bag."

"He lost it," said Morley from the kitchen.

"I need a note or I can't go," said Sam.

"You're telling us now?" asked Dave.

"I'll write the note," said Morley, throwing down the two lunch bags. Glowering. "You drive."

Forty minutes later, late himself, Dave is standing in front of the record store patting his pockets. In the rush to get the kids to school he has left the keys to the store at home. It is 10:30 before he opens.

◙ ◙ ◙

Tuesday Sam can't find his bike lock. He wants to use Stephanie's. Dave lurches into the yard, trying to get there before they start hitting each other.

"Stephanie won't let me use her lock," says the boy.

"He's lost his lock. That's his fault," says his sister.

Reaching for some cartons that are piled along the back wall of the garage, looking for an old lock that he is not even sure exists, Dave stumbles over the lawnmower and whacks his shin on something sharp. The pain crashes up his leg and settles behind his eyes. He moans out loud. The dog looks up at him, her tail wagging.

"Get out of here," he snarls. She has the good sense

to tuck her tail down and disappear.

Why is his garage such a goddamn mess? Even as he stands there he knows with certainty that no matter how much time he spent cleaning or ordering or hanging things on the wall it would always return to this. His family would always be late in the morning. His garage would always be a mess. If I could only find the god-damn lock, he thinks, it wouldn't bother me so much.

❋ ❋ ❋

At noon Morty Zuckerman phones the store and invites Dave and Morley to dinner on Friday night. The invitation catches Dave off guard. They hardly know the Zuckermans.

"We'd love to come," he says thinking as he hears himself say it, Why did I do that? It was against family rules. He was supposed to check. I should have checked, he thinks to himself as he hangs up.

❋ ❋ ❋

At supper Stephanie says she *needs* fifteen dollars.

"I can't find Elaine's tape. I have to buy her a new one."

"Maybe," says Dave, "you should use your own money."

"I don't want to use my money."

"Why not?"

"I don't want to waste *my* money on a tape for Elaine."

⊠ ⊠ ⊠

Lying in bed that night Dave puts his book down and flips off the lamp on his bedside table. He tucks his arms under his head.

"What are we doing wrong?" he asks his wife.

Morley, who has turned her light off only moments before, doesn't answer. She is already asleep.

⊠ ⊠ ⊠

On Thursday Dave gets a postcard from a regular customer—a young boy who, until recently, worked at the university radio station. He shopped for records at Dave's store. He left his job and the city to go to Alberta.

"I'm going Out West," he said.

The card is a picture of a Mountie and three native chiefs standing stiffly in front of a teepee. The Mountie is the only one smiling.

"Finally made it," reads the message, printed in red ink. "Have a job waiting in Jasper. At a ski lodge. Not sure doing what??? The sky is big out here. Have you heard Robbie Robertson's new album? Write."

It is the return address squeezed into the corner by the stamp that Dave reads twice: "General Delivery. Jasper, Alberta."

Dave had gone out west after his first year of university, sat up for two nights on the train, worked for two summers at the Jasper Park Lodge. Early one summer morning walking between the cabins on his way to the dining room where he worked as a waiter Dave walked right by Colonel Harland Sanders.

"Good-morning, Colonel," said Dave, not believing his eyes.

"Good-morning, son," said the Colonel.

He looked exactly the way he did in the television ads. Walking stick and all.

It seemed too long since Dave had moved with the sense of anticipation that surrounds you when you are on the road, and you know that there is a post office ahead of you where someone might have sent you a letter, a card.

No wonder the skies looked big.

At lunch Dave buys the cheesiest card he can of the city skyline and throws it in a mail box on the way home.

On it he has written: "There used to be a health food store with a pool table on the main street of Jasper. Is it still there? I used to go there and shoot pool and drink licorice tea. Sometimes travelling alone is scary. Everything will be all right. Have fun."

⊠ ⊠ ⊠

That night Dave dreams of a post office in the prairies. It is surrounded by wheat. In the dream Dave is standing in front of a wicket which has bars on it. It makes him think of a jail. It is unclear who is behind the bars. Dave? Or the man who is handing him the pack of letters? The letters are tied together with string. There is a woman waiting outside with a child in a stroller. The woman has a nice smile. Dave is holding out one of the letters. "It's my union card," he says to the woman. "I can get a job now." He feels proud. The woman says, "What about the fucking garage? When are you going to clean the garage?"

⊠ ⊠ ⊠

Morley phoned at noon and read to Dave from *The Globe and Mail.* An American tourist had been charged with assault in connection with the spanking of his five-year-old daughter in a London, Ontario, restaurant parking lot. The police said the man and his family had stopped for lunch when the girl had closed the car door on her sister's fingers. There were witnesses who said they saw the father pull down the girl's underwear, place her on the trunk of the car, and spank her with the palm of his hand. The police took the girl to hospital after the incident. A doctor didn't find any injuries.

"The incident! Jesus Christ," said Dave. "Do they really call it 'The Incident.'"

"Gotta go," said Morley.

Once, like the man in the newspaper, Dave had spanked both his children while they were on summer vacation. They were pulling out of New York City. Heading home on a hot August morning with a 500-mile drive in front of them. There was no air-conditioning in the car and though they had only been on the road for half an hour the kids were already acting up in the back seat. Somebody was going to hit somebody. I'd better nip this in the bud, Dave thought. He drove off the New York State Freeway and found himself circling the exit ramp and pulling into a housing development. It was early on a Sunday morning. There was a man mowing his lawn with a hand mower. Dave parked as far from the man as he could. He got out of the car and yanked the back door open. He reached in and pulled Stephanie out of the car and whacked her twice. Then he threw her back in and did the same to Sam.

There was a steamy silence for the next forty minutes and all Dave could think about as they smoked down the interstate was the cheerful wave from the man with the lawnmower as they peeled out of his neighbourhood.

What did it mean? Was it a wave of solidarity? Did cars of crazed families pull onto that street every day? Half an hour later it occurred to Dave that the man might have taken his licence plate number. Might have reported him to the authorities. Maybe the wave was a warning. Maybe the police were waiting for him at the border. Wouldn't that make this a vacation to remember?

About an hour later Sam said, "You shouldn't have done that."

Dave had the grace to say, "You're right."

◧ ◧ ◧

"Sam is going to sleep over at Ben's tomorrow night," said Morley on Thursday.

"Let's have a quiet night," said Dave. "Let's get a movie. I'll get some wine. We'll stay home. We'll order dinner."

◧ ◧ ◧

Friday night at 8:15 Morley and Dave are upstairs in the den snuggled on the couch.

"I told Stephanie to be home at 11:00," says Morley.

Morley is reading the paper. Dave peers at his wife over his book. He thinks to himself, She looks so beautiful. I am so lucky to be here on this couch with her. Sometimes the world is a perfect place. That is when he remembers the invitation to the Zuckermans'.

For a full frozen horrible minute he doesn't say anything.

It would be better for everyone, he thinks, if Morley doesn't know about this. He considers slipping down to the laundry room where there is a phone he can use without being heard. He would call the Zuckermans and say...what? That one of the kids was sick. No, it was too late for that. That one of the kids was dead. And they couldn't come. Or the babysitter was dead. No. There'd been an accident. He was...phoning from the hospital.

"We are," says Dave, achieving a calmness he did not feel, "Supposed to be at...uh...the Zuckermans'... eating dinner."

Morley doesn't say anything.

"Morty phoned on Tuesday. He asked us to dinner. Tonight. At seven o'clock."

"I didn't know this," says Morley. Ominously she is speaking even slower than Dave. "You didn't tell me this."

Dave is now worried more about himself than the Zuckermans.

"We were supposed to be there at seven," he says, glancing at his watch.

"It's not on the calendar, Dave. You didn't write it on the calendar." Morley sounds like Hal, the computer in the movie *2001*.

"What are you going to do about it?" she asks. Not *we*. Not what are *WE* going to do.

The Zuckermans live on Brock Avenue. Their house is less than a five-minute walk from Dave's house.

"I'll go over there," he says. "And look in the window. Maybe it's like a buffet. Maybe there are lots of people there. Maybe they haven't missed us."

"That's stupid Dave. Phone them."

"What?"

"Phone them."

"I can't phone them. If it's a buffet I don't have to phone them. A buffet is like a cocktail party. It doesn't matter when you arrive. It'll be OK. I'll be right back."

Dave is pleading.

"I'll be right back," he says. "Don't move."

When he gets there Dave looks at the Zuckermans' house from the far side of the street. The drapes are pulled.

"Now what?" he thinks.

But he knows now what.

He has to get closer.

He makes a tack by the house and then says, Now or never.

Glides over the front lawn like a spy, thinking, They won't see me in the dark. As long as I don't make a noise. As long as they don't have a dog. As long as a neighbour doesn't call the police. Jesus. How would he explain that? If the police arrived and Morty and Irene came outside and saw him being taken away. How could he explain skulking around their property when he was supposed to be inside eating? They would think he was crazy.

The windows at the side of the house are over Dave's head. There is a garbage can by the walk. Dave lugs it over to the window and then, holding onto the window sill, pulls himself up as if he was doing a chin-up. His head fills the window like a rising moon. He comes up about a foot away from Morty who is sitting by the window reading the paper. Irene is on the other side of the room. She is looking straight at him. Dave is sure she can see him. Ducks down, expecting a scream, leaves the garbage can where it is, runs for the street and doesn't stop running until he is around the block. Surely his father never did things like this. Christ, when is he going to grow up?

He meets Morley on the way home.

"We can't go there," he says. "They are just sitting there. They look like they have eaten."

"You don't have to come," says Morley. "But I'm going."

Dave follows his wife down the street. He is a step behind her.

"Listen," he says frantically. "I have an idea. Why don't we go tomorrow night instead? We show up at seven o'clock tomorrow. That would cover it. They'll know we had it wrong. But they won't know for sure. There'll be doubt. They'll at least have to *wonder* if Morty made a mistake."

Morley keeps walking.

"Or we don't go at all. And we never mention it. Pretend it never happened. Listen, we can invite them over to our house in like three weeks. Anything. With other people. To show that we like them."

Morley keeps walking.

"Or phone them. Let's go back home and phone them and you can say I've had a heart attack. For God's sake, Morley, it's too late to go."

Morley stops and turns and repeats the only thing she has said since her husband came back.

"You don't have to come if you don't want to. But I'm going."

What could he say to that? What else could he do but keep walking. Following his wife like a boy on a shopping trip with his mother. Only moments ago he was totally in love with her. Now as he struggles to keep up he hears himself silently invoking the Lord to bring down a bolt of lightning and strike her dead at his feet so he won't have to keep going. Won't have to stand on his neighbour's porch beside her. Won't have to live through the rest of the night. In fact, he thinks, looking up, if a bolt of lightning did come down he could phone the Zuckermans from the hospital and say he was sorry they hadn't made it to dinner but on the way over Morley had been hit by lightning and he was phoning from the hospital.

When they get there, when they are standing on the porch and Morley's hand is moving towards the doorbell Dave says, "I'm sorry. This is my fault. I'm sorry."

"Yes," she says. "This is your fault."

Then she rings the bell.

"What are we going to say?" asks Dave.

"I phoned already," she says. "I phoned while you were gone."

Irene Zuckerman is smiling when she opens the door.

STANLEY

If it wasn't for her dog, Dorothy Capper might have ended up married to Albert Sugerman. Dorothy bought the dog, a golden retriever, in 1978, two months after her first husband, George, left home to live with one of his students. For a week or two Dorothy toyed with the idea of naming the dog after him. The possibilities pleased her.

"I have to go home and walk George," she imagined herself saying, her lip curled.

"George dirtied the rug last night," she snorted one morning at breakfast. She was alone, eating corn flakes and drinking tea. The idea cracked her up. She laughed, out loud.

Or calling him. That was good. George come here. Here George. George-George-George-George-George.

And, Bad-Dog-George. Bad-dog. Get out of here, George. You asshole.

Once she had the dog in her house she couldn't go through with it. She settled on Stanley instead. After the great Canadian parliamentarian Stanley Knowles. When Dorothy was a university student in Winnipeg she lived in Stanley Knowles' riding. Her politics were changed forever the electrifying night she heard Tommy Douglas and Stanley Knowles at an NDP rally during the 1963 election. It was Knowles, by then almost sixty years old, who taught her about American involvement in South-east Asia. It was Knowles, not her university friends, who led her on her first protest march. Knowles became her all-time hero when someone told her he was the only Canadian parliamentarian to dissent when Canada declared war on Germany in 1939. That was why she named the dog after him. Later she learned that Knowles wasn't elected to parliament until 1942. That it was his mentor, James Woodsworth, "the conscience of Canada," who had stood up and tried to persuade Mackenzie King's government to declare neutrality. It was Woodsworth who had said, "War only breeds war."

So when she opened her bookstore she named it Woodsworth's. She couldn't very well change Stanley's name. He was four years old.

Dorothy knew exactly what she was doing buying the dog. It wasn't for company—although, at the time, the notion of having something in her life that loved and, more importantly, listened to her, was a comforting thought. She bought him because she didn't want her life getting too easy. Complications were important. Without something messing up your plans you became self-centred. Then you became selfish.

Albert Sugerman was a complication.

He was a book rep who worked for H.B. Fenn. He came into her store three times a year with his catalogues to flog the next season's list. What was refreshing about Albert Sugerman was that, unlike most of the reps who visited her, he did not pretend to be interested in books. Albert loved sales. He had previously sold cars, wholesale cosmetics, chemicals and gravel.

One night, over dinner, he told Dorothy what frustrated him about selling books was that bookstores had to buy from him regardless of his skill.

"For example, when I had the Madonna book." He said this with a rueful glance. The Madonna book was a favourite of Albert's. It was more a magazine than a book, a sealed portfolio of pop star nudie shots. But it flew off the shelves into the arms of people who ordinarily never thought about going into bookstores. The idea of sealing the book, so you had to buy it to see inside, an idea which flew in the face of book-selling convention, staggered Albert with its brilliance.

"Man," he said to Dorothy once, "...perfect."

"Anyway. When I had Madonna, bookstores were going to take it regardless of what I did. Because if they don't take it from me they don't get it. And everyone wanted it. And that makes this a service business. I'm a serviceman. Not a salesman."

"I didn't take it," said Dorothy.

"Didn't take it?"

"Madonna. It wasn't a book."

"Doesn't matter. We sold the entire run anyway. Doesn't matter if you and a bunch of purists pass. It all went anyway."

"Wouldn't it have been a challenge to get some into my store?" She was playing with him.

Albert said he hadn't tried.

Dorothy said, "Why don't you?"

After dinner he went back to her place for coffee and didn't leave until the morning.

That was the autumn of 1993.

Albert was the second man in her life since George had left. The first was a computer programmer named Max. A man who even Dorothy came to think of as too idiosyncratic. They also met in the store. Max was a regular customer. He came in on Friday nights near closing and took to staying after she locked the door. They would talk while she tidied up. Going for coffee seemed like the most natural thing in the world. Getting him into bed was a challenge. Dorothy felt odd in the role of aggressor. They dated for two years. And finally split up on the telephone. Which was strange because Max didn't have a phone at home.

"I have one at work," he said. "I don't understand the need of having one at home."

Dorothy explained that it would be nice if she could call him from time to time. If she wanted to do something maybe she could call him, and they could do something?

Max said, "I had a phone once. And you know what I learned? If you let a phone into your house the damn thing just starts to ring. People think, 'Here's something that needs to be done. Let's call Max.' It's remarkable how seldom you get calls that you really want."

Dorothy said, "You could get an answering machine."

Max said, "I have an answering machine at work."

Dorothy used to go to Max's apartment and they would watch videos together. The night they first made love Max cooked dinner for her—trout amandine and rice. After they ate he turned on his karaoke machine and sang for her. Dorothy sat on the couch and he stood in the middle of the living-room and sang "Raindrops Keep Falling On My Head" by Burt Bacharach and "This Guy's In Love With You." "Herb Alpert did that one," he said. Then he said, "I've never sung to anyone before." Dorothy said, "It's a first for me too."

Sometimes they went to the theatre or the symphony. Sometimes they went to a Thai restaurant on Eglinton Avenue.

One night she said, "What about your parents?"

Max said, "My parents?"

Dorothy said, "Your parents and the phone."

Max said, "It drives them crazy. They say, 'What if we need to get you in a hurry?'"

She watched him ladle the end of the Thai soup into his bowl. He didn't ask if she wanted more.

"What they mean," she said, "is, 'What if one of us dies?'"

"Yeah. I know what they mean," said Max.

"Well," she said, "what if one of them dies?"

"What can I do about that?" said Max.

They broke up two weeks later.

▣ ▣ ▣

"Did you know your dog snores?" said Albert the morning he stayed over for the first time.

It was an understatement of staggering proportions. Stanley didn't just snore. Sleeping in the same bedroom as Stanley was like sleeping beside a working band saw.

The dog slept on the floor at the end of the bed. With each buzzing inhalation Albert imagined he could hear cupboard doors in the kitchen flapping on their hinges, imagined the rocking chair in the living-room teetering back and forth, thought he heard the bureau drawers in the bedroom being sucked open and closed, open and closed. For two awful hours Albert lay in bed listening while the dog gasped and gulped, until unexpectedly there was a loud arrhythmic snort, like an explosion. The snort was followed by a profound silence. It was as if the dog had abruptly stopped breathing. Albert propped himself up on his elbows and tried to peer over his feet to the floor at the foot of the bed. He didn't want to wake Dorothy who, amazingly, didn't seem to be having any trouble sleeping. It was too dark to see anything. Albert held his breath and let himself down slowly onto his pillow. For the first time all night he could hear Dorothy breathing sweetly beside him. He watched the red numbers on the clock radio blink from 2:37 to 2:38 to 2:39. He closed his eyes. He wondered if he should have stayed the night.

Then he wondered if he should stay for breakfast. Maybe he should leave early, get a paper, eat at the Mars diner by himself. He started to think about his own bed, about his pyjamas, about something blue and soft. His mind was filled by a sense of blueness, but he was beyond trying to understand what it was. Maybe it was a boat, or maybe it was a smell, or maybe a feeling, a floating feeling. He was falling asleep. And he was totally unprepared for what happened next.

The silences, he would later learn, could last as long as twenty or thirty minutes, but they always ended with a whooshing explosion that sounded more like a whale breaching than anything Albert had ever heard coming out of a dog. When it happened the first time, this time, when Albert was thinking about something blue, it nearly drove him through the ceiling. There was a gust of noise and he gasped and sat up and said, "Sweet Jesus." He thought he was about to be squashed by some huge Blue Thing.

He could feel his heart racing.

"Christ," he said.

It took twenty minutes for Albert's heart to slow down. He was still awake, lying there as stiff as a sheet of plywood, when Stanley snorted and stopped snoring for the second time. Lying there in the darkness waiting for Stanley to start up again nearly drove Albert mad.

Dorothy had been sleeping with Stanley for twelve years. She didn't notice a thing.

Dorothy took Stanley with her to the store every morning. He passed most of each day on an old piece of blanket near the cash register. People seemed to like having a dog in the store. Enough customers mentioned it that Dorothy had come to believe that Stanley had something to do with whatever small success she had found over the years. She wasn't a superstitious person but there was some superstition blended with the love she felt for him.

Albert, however, was having trouble coming to terms with the dog. Whenever he stayed over he only slept fitfully. He always left Dorothy's place exhausted.

One day on the subway he saw an ad for laser surgery.

"What about laser surgery?" he asked. "Do you think they could do the laser surgery on dogs?"

Two weeks later Albert returned to the subway station with a pencil and paper. He copied down the clinic's number and called them from the office.

"I'm phoning about the snoring operation," he said. "Could you send me some literature. A pamphlet or something?"

"We don't have any pamphlets," said the woman. "But I could book you an appointment. You come for a consultation. If you want to proceed there is a sleep study and then the operation. Everything is covered by OHIP except the operation. The operation is $1,200."

"Do you do dogs?" asked Albert. "It's the dog who snores. Not me."

There was an unpleasant pause.

"No," said the lady. "We don't do dogs."

"Are you sure?" asked Albert. She was, after all, only the receptionist. "Could you check?"

The woman covered the phone but Albert could hear her.

"Jane, do we do dogs?"

He couldn't hear Jane.

"No," said the woman, uncovering the phone. "We don't do dogs. You'd have to go to a vet for dogs."

"But a vet wouldn't have the laser," said Albert, peevishly.

One Saturday Albert turned up at Dorothy's house with a device he had bought at a drug store for ten dollars. It was called the Nozovent. It was a small horseshoe-shaped piece of plastic designed to cure snoring. The instruction booklet said that controlled clinical trials had shown the elimination of snoring in about one-third of the people who had tried the Nozovent. Albert said he was going to put the Nozovent up Stanley's nose. The instruction booklet didn't mention dogs.

When they were ready for bed Albert got down on the living-room floor and called Stanley. He had a dog biscuit in one hand and the Nozovent in the other. Stanley, who wasn't used to getting much attention from Albert, sniffed the cookie suspiciously. Albert put the Nozovent in his mouth so he had both hands free and grabbed Stanley by the collar. He pulled the dog towards him. Stanley dug his paws into the carpet and yelped. Albert pulled harder. Stanley started to growl. As he wrestled with the dog, Albert's hand slipped between its collar and its neck—up to the wrist—and it stuck there. No matter how hard he pulled, his hand wouldn't come out. The pressure of Albert's hand against his neck seemed to panic Stanley. He began to snap at Albert's arm. Albert thought, Christ, I am in a dog fight. I am going to get bitten. He wondered if Stanley had had his rabies shots. The idea of rabies scared him and he tried to roll away but he pulled Stanley with him. The dog flew over his head and they landed in a heap, against the sofa, Stanley's back leg resting against Albert's face. In that unexpected quiet moment Albert looked at the dog's leg and considered biting it. Maybe it would establish his dominance over the dog. If he did that he could do what he liked with his hand—which was to get it out from under the collar before he got bitten and got rabies. Albert did not want to have a series of rabies shots in his stomach. But before he could open his mouth Stanley beat him to the punch. The dog snapped at his arm and this time got a mouthful of flesh. Albert heard a sound come out of his own mouth that he didn't recognize. The sound scared him more than the pain in his arm. He pushed the dog as hard as he could, twisted his arm and rolled backwards like a commando. As he rolled he inhaled and accidently swallowed the Nozovent. Cracky, he thought as he landed on his knees. The two of them, the dog and the salesman, had ended up on opposite sides of the living-room. Albert was kneeling, as if he was praying, his hand on his chest trying to feel for the Nozovent. His shirt was out. His mouth open. The Nozovent had gone down so smoothly it worried him. He wondered if he should go to the hospital. Then he remembered his arm. He looked to see if the flesh had been broken. Stanley had both paws extended out in front of him. His tail was wagging.

"How's it coming?" called Dorothy from the bedroom.

"Do you know," said Albert pointedly two weeks later, "that the Guinness Book of World Records snoring champion lives in Vancouver."

Dorothy didn't know this.

"You know how loud he snores?" Albert wasn't expecting an answer.

"Ninety decibels. That's the equivalent of sleeping beside a pneumatic drill."

It was the first time Albert had ever read to Dorothy.

"I don't hear him," she said.

"They tested his wife," said Albert. "And she has experienced serious hearing loss."

"So?"

"Because of the snoring."

"So?"

"Maybe that's why you don't hear him."

Dorothy *wasn't* bothered by the snoring. And if truth be known there were things about Albert that were beginning to get under her skin. She didn't like his taste in movies. Or that he always chose what they watched. She didn't like the fact that he didn't read.

"You sell books. You should read one occasionally."

One Sunday morning Albert, unshaven and exhausted, said, "It's either the dog or me."

Dorothy felt a great sense of freedom wash over her. She looked at Albert and didn't say anything.

"Hey. Come on," he said. "I don't believe this."

■ ■ ■

Stanley developed his digestive problems the next summer. It started innocuously enough but by August he would lie by the cash register at the store emitting an intolerable stream of gas—so rank that sometimes the store smelled like there was a moose carcass rotting behind the shelves.

It wouldn't have been so bad if Stanley had just ripped the odd loud fart. The problem was that he snuck them out. Like he was ashamed of them.

"And well he should be," said Dorothy to a friend one afternoon.

Dorothy realized she had to do something about Stanley's problem when customers began glaring at her. They think it's me, she thought.

The vet was encouraging.

"It's something in his diet," he said.

But after three months of juggling dog foods the

vet gave up.

"I don't know," he said. "Maybe you should put him down."

Dorothy was horrified.

She told the vet that when Stanley Knowles had a stroke no one suggested they put him to sleep.

The vet said, "Stanley Knowles, the politician?"

Dorothy said, "Yes."

The vet said, "What has Stanley Knowles got to do with anything?"

Dorothy said, "When Stanley Knowles retired they named him an honorary Officer of the House of Commons with a place for life at the Clerk's Table."

The vet didn't say anything.

Dorothy said, "Forget it. How much do I owe you?"

It was her friend Vicky who said, "Stop feeding him meat."

Dorothy said, "But that's all dogs eat."

Vicky said, "I'm telling you, stop feeding him meat."

Dorothy found a pet food store that sold vegetarian dog food. HEALTHY PETS it was called. She felt silly going into what was essentially a health food store for animals but decided to try it for a month.

Stanley wasn't ecstatic about his new diet. He didn't eat anything for the first week.

"Don't give up," said Vicky. "He'll come around."

Eventually he did. And, eventually, it worked.

"Who would have guessed," Dorothy said to Vicky.

"Me," said Vicky.

Stanley was eating again but he was not happy. He spent most of his waking hours on meat patrol. Walking him was like taking a vacuum cleaner for a stroll. He kept his nose to the ground and sucked up anything that resembled food.

However, the gas had virtually disappeared and Stanley did seem livelier than he had in years.

"Hungrier too," said Albert, who had stayed friends with Dorothy even though they had stopped seeing each other. Albert was living with a vegetarian himself and used to show up and take Dorothy to lunch.

"Let's have shish-kebab," he would say.

Not having to sleep with Stanley any more he felt a sense of kinship with the dog he had never felt before.

When Stanley was sixteen Dorothy knew the end was drawing near. He had developed arthritis in his hips and his gums were giving him problems. That meant walking was hard and so was eating.

"What else does a dog do for fun?" asked Dorothy.

"Maybe it's time to put him down," said Albert one day at lunch. He had taken her out for smoked meat on Spadina Avenue.

Dorothy looked at him.

"I could do it," he said. "I could take him out to my brother's farm and I'll...I can...like...we can...he's got guns and things. You know."

Dorothy didn't say anything.

"Think about it," said Albert. "It would be in the country. I'd be with you. He knows me. Christ. We used to sleep together."

When they got back to the store Albert squatted down beside Stanley, petting his head.

Shit, thought Dorothy.

Two months later Stanley had a stroke. Dorothy had to hold him when he was walking upstairs. Had to put her arms under his chest and take the weight off his feet. Their walks got shorter and shorter. And slower. It was like walking with a two-year-old. Everything about Stanley was slowing down. He wanted to be beside her all the time. As if he was scared. Confused. She couldn't take him to the store any more.

She phoned Albert.

"OK," she said.

Albert came on Saturday morning. He had a blanket on the back seat of his car.

"I'm not coming," said Dorothy.

Albert said, "You sure?"

Dorothy said, "Yes."

Albert moved the blanket into the front seat and they carried Stanley out and Dorothy said, "At least he doesn't have to go to the vet."

She scratched her dog behind the ears and said, "See you. Good dog."

Albert said, "I'm going now."

Dorothy said, "OK."

He gave her a hug and drove away.

When he got to Orangeville Albert stopped at McDonald's and bought himself a Big Mac, a vanilla shake and an order of fries. He got it to go.

Stanley, who had been sleeping beside him on the front seat, woke up as soon as he opened the burger and Albert thought, What the hell, and slipped him a bite. The dog's tail started to thump on the seat. He looked so grateful for the meat that Albert said, "Shit," and drove onto the shoulder and waited for the traffic to clear. He made a U-turn and headed back to Orangeville. When he got to the McDonald's he ordered four Big Macs. "No, five," he said, into the speaker.

He ate one himself and fed two to Stanley during the hour it took them to get to the farm.

He gave Stanley a third when they got there. And another on the grass behind the barn where he took him with his brother. The dog let out a long loud happy fart when he finished it, and sighed, and seemed to be falling asleep as Albert's brother handed him the gun.

DRIVING LESSONS

orley was telling her friend Nicky about her mother's accident. They were talking on the telephone. They were both fixing supper as they talked.

"Just a second," Morley said. "Wait a minute. Wait a minute. Shoot."

There was a crash as the receiver snapped off Morley's shoulder.

Nicky winced.

"What's the matter?" she asked.

It sounded like the phone had fallen into the blender. "What's happening?"

What was happening was that the receiver was snaking across the kitchen floor. The dog was chasing it.

"Morley?"

There was another clatter. Then Morley came back on the line.

"Sorry," she said.

"What happened?"

"The potatoes were boiling over. Where was I?"

"Your mother."

"She rear ended someone. It wasn't her fault. Someone jumped out in front of the guy and he slammed on his brakes."

"Was she hurt?"

"No. No. She's OK."

"What about the other guy?"

"No. Everyone was OK. It was Friday night. She came here after it happened. Dave and I were supposed to be going out. She got here the same time as the babysitter."

"How?"

"How what?"

"How'd she get there?"

"She drove."

"Did you go out?"

"Yeah. It was her second accident since Christmas."

"What did you do?"

"What do you mean what did we do?"

"Where did you go?"

"We went to a movie. I'm worried she's going to kill someone."

"I wish *my* mother could still drive. What did you see?"

"I don't remember. Damn. What did we see? The one with the guy and the bomb. Where the father gets blown up. You know, that's the problem. Everyone is so impressed because she is eighty-two years old and she still has her mind. She also has cataracts. She can hardly see, Nicky. She's going to kill someone."

"Don't they have to take the test when they're over eighty?"

"She took the test. She's waiting for cataract surgery and you know what the guy said? He said, 'I am going to retire in seven years and if I can drive as well as you can when I'm sixty-five I'll be happy.'"

"He passed her?"

"Yeah he passed her."

"So don't worry."

"She's had two accidents since Christmas."

"You said it wasn't her fault."

"Still."

◪ ◪ ◪

"If you're so worried. Why don't you call the police?"

Morley and Dave were lying in bed.

"She's my own mother. How can I turn my mother in? I can't rat on my own mother. What if I call and she finds out about it?"

"What if you don't and she kills someone?"

"Thanks, Dave. That's a big help. Thanks a lot. Why don't *you* call the cops."

"She's not my mother."

"Great. That's great. That's really great."

Morley was picking up her pillows and heading out of the room.

"Well she isn't," said Dave as she disappeared.

She was going to sleep on the couch.

◪ ◪ ◪

Dave said, "I'm sorry."

Morley didn't say, "It's OK."

Dave said, "Listen. She hardly drives any more. What does she do? She goes for groceries. How far is it to the grocery store? A quarter of a mile? Two turns? She goes to bridge. Those are the sort of trips you could do in your pyjamas. Who's going to see you? What's going to happen?"

"I know what's going to happen," said Morley. "She's going to kill someone, Dave. That's what's going to happen."

"She's not going to kill someone going to the grocery store."

"You know what happened last month? She got lost. You know where she got lost? She got lost in Scarborough."

"Scarborough?"

"She went to dinner at Norah's house and she got lost coming home. She said she didn't know where she was. She said she couldn't see the numbers on the houses or read the signs. She said she was so scared she was shaking. And then she got on the highway, don't ask me how, somehow she found the highway, but she didn't know where she was going. And you know what she told me? She said she must have been driving funny because someone stopped and helped her. Someone stopped, Dave. She said they told her she was going the wrong way."

"I thought she didn't drive at night."

"How else was she supposed to get there?"

"She could have taken the subway. The subway goes

to Scarborough."

"She hates the subway. The stairs are too hard."

"But she figured it out. Anyone could get lost in Scarborough. She got home. Right? She's fine."

"You know what scares me, Dave? She said she was heading the wrong way—going the wrong way. I don't know whether she meant she was heading in the wrong direction or driving on the wrong side of the highway."

"Did you ask her?"

"I was too scared to ask her. Somebody stopped. What do you think?"

🞑 🞑 🞑

Dave was reading the paper. Morley was knitting.

Dave said, "Did you know some guy in Kansas, some eighty-year-old guy in Lawrence, Kansas, has Albert Einstein's brain in a pickle jar in his apartment?"

Morley said, "No. Mom phoned today."

Dave said, "The guy was a pathologist. And he was on duty when Einstein died so he did the autopsy and kept the brain so he could study it. What did she want?"

Morley said, "Nothing. Every time she leaves a message on the machine I feel guilty erasing it."

Dave said, "Listen. 'The most celebrated brain of the twentieth century resides in Apartment 13 on the second floor of a nondescript brick apartment building here.' Here is Lawrence. Kansas. The guy has it all cut up. He says he is two-thirds of the way through studying it."

Morley said, "I keep thinking it'll turn out to be the last thing she ever says to me and I will have erased it."

Dave said, "He keeps it in his hall closet."

Morley said, "I invited her for dinner on Friday. It's Dad's birthday."

Dave said, "Friday?"

Morley said, "When did Einstein die anyway?"

Dave said, "1955."

Morley said, "How?"

Dave said, "Automobile accident. He was hit by an old lady."

Morley said "What?"

Dave said, "Just kidding. It doesn't say. It just says he was seventy-five."

⊠ ⊠ ⊠

There is a picture of her father on Morley's bureau. It is in a gold frame. It was taken in Florida ten years ago. Roy was seventy-six years old. He looks impossibly young and vigorous. The sun in his face, the wind tugging at his hair. He is squinting.

"Thirty years as a copper," he used to say, "and the pay-off is I get to go to Florida and squint for three months."

Ten years ago Helen and Roy used to drive to Florida and back and didn't even think about it. Nobody thought about it.

They brought back pictures of their friends, all of

them holding drinks, standing around someone's mobile home—it's not a trailer park, Helen used to say, mobile homes, mobile homes. When she saw those pictures Morley used to think, who's the young guy? Then she'd realize it was him, Roy, her father.

Six years ago, in January, he collapsed. Helen phoned and said, "You better get down here." She said it was like someone unplugged him. Dave said, "What do the doctors say?"

Morley phoned the hospital in Clearwater and spoke to a doctor and he said, "You have to be philosophical about this, he has had a good life." Morley and Dave rushed down and put the trailer up for sale and sold some stuff and left the rest of it for whoever bought it, for whatever they wanted to pay.

After two weeks the doctors said he could travel. Dave had already left with the car. Morley flew back with them. She couldn't believe how old Roy looked. He could walk but he was walking old. He didn't seem to be paying attention to anything. He didn't want to eat.

Roy had always been so strong.

When he was a young man he played hockey. In 1927 he played centre for the Toronto Granites. It was three years after the Granites won the gold medal at the Winter Olympics.

He was a born athlete. He used to go and watch the Maple Leafs play baseball at the Hanlan's Point Stadium. He took his glove. If he got there early enough they would let him shag flies during batting practice.

He quit school when he was sixteen and worked on an ice truck. Two years later the hockey team got him a job at the Inglis factory on Strachan Avenue. He stayed there, working in shipping and then on the line, for almost fifteen years.

When he and Helen got married they got a place in the suburbs and he used to run a mile every morning to the end of the streetcar line so he wouldn't have to pay two fares. In those days when you changed cars you had to pay a second fare.

He got a weekend job with the Mounties and when the war came they hired him full time. They gave him a rifle and one bullet and sent him to Port Colborne to guard the Welland Canal. He wasn't allowed to put the bullet in the rifle in case he hurt someone. He used to say it was the most boring job he ever had.

Dave tried to tease him about it once. He said, "But you must have been good at it, Roy, you must have done a great job. At no point in the war did the Nazis make it anywhere near the canal." Roy looked at him as if he was nuts. He wasn't going to let anyone say the job was unnecessary.

After the war Roy left Inglis and got a job with the North York police force. It paid less than the factory but it was with the township and that meant job security. There were only fifteen other men on the force when he joined. When he retired there were three hundred and he was an inspector.

⊠ ⊠ ⊠

When they got back from Florida, Morley took Roy to see Dr. Freeberg and she said, "I want you to go and see a blood specialist." The blood specialist asked Roy to walk across the room and he diagnosed him before he got to the other side. It was his thyroid. He gave him a prescription and said, "Take these and you will feel better in three days." He took his first pill at the drug store and started feeling better on the way home. "Those goddamn American doctors," said Morley.

But he was never the same. He was like a balloon with the air slowly seeping out of it. Sometimes when he and Helen came for dinner he would sit in the living-room as if he was the only one there. Other times he was bright and chatty, telling them what was in the paper, what he had seen on the news. He still did the crossword every day.

He kept driving but he was nervous about it. He got a speeding ticket—45 km in a 35-km zone. He was incensed. It was his first violation. Ever.

One day they were in the garage downstairs on their way to the supermarket and he was revving the engine and Helen said, "What are you doing?" And he said, "I'm backing out. Why?" And she said, "Why don't you put it in reverse first?" It was just a lapse. He was thinking about something else. But it worried him. "I want to keep driving," he told Dave. "I couldn't stand it if I couldn't drive."

Another time he was pulling into the parking lot at the back of the apartment and he hit one of the huge plastic garbage cans lined up in the alley.

Dave said, "I could have done that, Roy. Don't worry about it."

But he worried.

Then one day he phoned Dave at work and said, "I'm at the liquor store. You better come and get me."

Roy had gone to the store to pick up a case of pop and a dozen eggs and some orange juice. When he was pulling out of his parking spot he put the Buick into reverse instead of forward.

"I don't know," he said. "I just did it."

When he pressed the accelerator the car lurched backwards instead of going the way he expected it to go. Roy said it felt like the car had been possessed by a demon and the only thing he could think of was to press harder on the accelerator. He didn't figure out what had happened until he hit the car behind him. It was a little red Honda.

Instead of getting out of his car and checking the damage, he took off.

"I don't know," he said. "I guess I was thinking they might take my licence away or something. All I could think about was that I had to get out of there. If I would have stopped..."

"I know," said Dave.

STUART McLEAN

When he pulled up to the stop sign at the parking lot exit Roy checked his rear-view mirror and, to his horror, saw that the Honda was right on his bumper. The guy in the Honda was shaking his fist at him.

"He wasn't thinking straight," said Dave to Morley. "He was scared of losing his licence. He was scared of being old."

"I know," said Morley.

As soon as there was a break in the traffic Roy roared out onto Dupont Avenue.

"I never drove that fast in the city in my life," he said.

"Even when you were a cop?" said Dave.

"I don't know," said Roy.

When he checked his mirror and saw the guy in the Honda was still behind him—and not just following him but right up against him—Roy thought, the bastard thinks he can tailgate me. I'll show him. He took the corner at Howland Avenue almost on two wheels and the Honda came screaming around the corner right on his bumper. Roy thought, Christ this is crazy. He sped up.

He kept checking the mirror as he went down Howland and that's when he noticed the guy in the Honda was still waving at him. In fact he wasn't only waving he was pounding on his windshield. With both hands. Roy thought, How's he doing that? Driving so fast and so close to me without using his hands. Which is when he realized the guy in the Honda *wasn't* driving. *Roy* was doing the driving. The Honda was hooked onto his bumper. Roy was dragging the Honda through the middle of Toronto like a fish on a line.

"I can't believe this," said Dave. "What was the guy doing?"

"He just kept banging on the windshield," said Roy.

Instead of stopping Roy decided to try and shake him loose.

"I turned around and waved at him," said Roy. "And I started weaving from side to side. Jerking the wheel like. Slowing down and speeding up."

"You waved at him?" said Dave.

"And smiled like," said Roy.

"He must have thought you were crazy. He must have thought he was going to die."

"I think that's when he started honking the horn," said Roy.

The two cars finally separated when Roy took the corner at Barton. He saw the Honda fly off across the sidewalk and stop against a tree.

"He didn't hit too hard," said Roy.

"Was he hurt?" asked Dave.

"I don't think so," he said.

Roy hadn't stopped to check.

Instead of hanging around, Roy drove to the liquor store and bought himself a pint of Jack Daniels and phoned Dave and said, "You better come and pick me up." When Dave arrived, Roy was sitting in the passenger seat of his car. Dave watched him for a moment—saw him take a swig of the Jack Daniels—watched him fingering the dashboard as if he was saying goodbye.

When he saw him, Roy handed his keys to Dave and said, "You drive it home."

■ ■ ■

Morley said, "You know what I thought today. I thought I should get a tape recorder and leave it by the phone so I could record all her messages on a tape before I erased them. Then I wouldn't have to worry."

Dave said, "About what? What messages?"

Morley said, "Helen's messages. I could record them all onto a tape. Then I wouldn't feel bad erasing them. I could keep them all on a tape. It would be like a diary."

■ ■ ■

Roy died in 1987. And still, all the time, Helen catches herself thinking, I have to tell that to Roy. She sees something, or reads something, and she thinks, Roy would like that. And then she remembers, Roy is dead. It's such a black, empty, feeling.

On Friday at supper she says, "I saw a program about the invasion. On TV. When you hear that the invasion was fifty years ago—you just don't believe it. It feels so strange."

Stephanie says, "What invasion?"

Sam says, "Can I be excused?"

■ ■ ■

After supper Helen wants to help with the dishes and Morley lets her, even though she knows they'll fight about it. Knows she will hand something back and say it is still dirty and her mother will get huffy. Promises herself not to do it but Helen hands her a plate that is so greasy she can't bear the idea of wiping it with the towel and she says, "Mother, could you rinse that a little more, please." She tries to be offhand about it but Helen says, "I know how to wash dishes. You don't have to tell me how to wash dishes."

When she was young Morley could be as mean to her mother as she wanted. It was part of her job description. Now Helen is more fragile. Delicate. The repercussions of anger are much greater than they used to be.

"I washed more dishes in my life than you'll ever wash," says Helen, rubbing the plate harder than necessary.

She is scared, thinks Morley. She feels like she is losing control. That's why she gets so angry. She doesn't even know how she is behaving. If I get mad back it will feel like my anger has come out of nowhere.

Their roles were changing and both of them resented it.

The first time she noticed it, two, three years ago, Morley had gone to Helen's apartment to pick her up. They were going to meet Dave for dinner and then to a show. Standing in the hallway, holding her mother's coat, Morley saw a stain on her green dress—Helen couldn't see it—but she would have been horrified to know it was there. Morley didn't say anything.

She is my mother, thought Morley. I am not supposed to look after her. She is supposed to look after me. Except Morley didn't want a mother any more. Bristled every time Helen told her how to do something or kissed her good night. And found it maddening when Helen wouldn't accept her help.

"She wants to be independent," said Dave. "She doesn't understand dependency."

That was what the car was all about. If Helen stopped driving, her world would become smaller. And it would never become larger again. Morley wanted her mother's world to become more restricted. But she understood why it terrified her.

When Roy had given up driving, Morley had tried to persuade Helen to quit too.

Helen had said, "How would we get around? I don't walk well any more. My back bothers me. I can't walk and carry stuff at the same time."

Dave said, "What about the subway?"

Helen said, "I can't take the subway. All those stairs."

Morley said, "Sell the car. With the money you save from insurance and gas and repairs you could afford to take taxis. You could take taxis anywhere."

"How would we get to the supermarket?" said Helen. As if it couldn't be done.

"Taxi," said Dave.

"But how," said Roy triumphantly, "would we get home?"

To a man who used to run a mile every day to save a

five-cent streetcar fare the idea of taking two taxis in one day was unthinkable.

❂ ❂ ❂

Helen stayed over on Friday night. After she did the dishes she watched television.

"I saw a special on the invasion the other night," she said. "It's so hard to believe it was only fifty years ago. Roy would have liked it."

❂ ❂ ❂

It was two months later that Helen found the old clipping. She was in a sorting mode—going through some old papers when she came across an announcement that someone had clipped from the police newsletter. At first it confused her. It said that her father had won the Policeman of the Month Award. But it wasn't her father who had won that—it was Roy. She couldn't make sense of the clipping. Had she got her father and her husband mixed up in her mind? She started to get scared. Then she saw the date on the clipping. April 1912. She suddenly understood that both her father and Roy must have won the same award—at different times. She remembered when Roy had won. They had gone out to dinner at a restaurant and a man had taken their picture at their table. She wondered what had happened to the photo. God, she wished Roy was here. She wanted him to know this. She wished they could tell her father. She looked at the clipping again and she felt her heart sink. There was no one left to tell. No one who would appreciate it. Anyone who knew her father would know what a thrill it would have given him to know this. He was so proud when Roy had joined the force. She thought, I hope he knows. She thought, I hope he and Roy both know. She started to cry. She thought, I wish I had someone to tell.

She phoned Morley and said, "Can I come over? I have something I want to show you."

She didn't say what it was.

It was four o'clock.

The early spring sun was low in the sky. As she turned west onto Roxborough she squinted and reached for the visor. When she came to the cross-walk the sun was still in her eyes and she didn't see the man step off the sidewalk, his arm extended. Only heard the sickening thump when she hit him. Only saw him lying in a heap on the road in the rear-view mirror. She stopped the car and struggled with the seat-belt and ran back to help him, but some young men had appeared from somewhere and pushed her away and said, "We don't need you here." She felt sick. She felt like she was going to faint. She went back to her car and started to cry and a nice woman came and sat beside her. She said, "Could I call someone for you?" Helen said, "No, it's OK." The woman stayed with her until the police came. Helen told her the story of the clipping. Told her how both her husband and her father had won the same police award and that neither of them knew it. All the time she kept twisting in her seat trying to see the man. Wishing he would sit up. She started to shake when she saw them take him away in an ambulance. A policeman came over and she said, "My husband was a policeman. Is the man all right?" The policeman didn't know. He said he wasn't going to take her licence. He said she might have to take the test again.

She made herself drive to Morley's. After dinner Dave phoned all the hospitals for her and they said there had been no serious accidents and that gave her hope.

She stayed two days. She fussed a little in the kitchen but mostly she watched television. She didn't talk a lot.

"I'm worried," said Morley.

"She'll be OK," said Dave.

On Wednesday when Dave came home from work she had gone home.

"She left this afternoon," said Morley. "She came down after lunch and said she had to get going."

"Did you drive her?" said Dave.

"She drove herself."

"Huh. I didn't think you'd let her."

"She said she was scared to drive. Then she said, 'But old age isn't for sissies.' What could I say to that, Dave?"

FRESH,
NEVER FROZEN

n Wednesday, Margaret Dwyer promised herself she would tell her husband that she had been caught shoplifting at the supermarket. She would tell him after supper. She had put it off for three and a half weeks, but she couldn't put it off any longer. If *she* didn't tell him he was going to find out. The kids knew. They hadn't mentioned anything but Margaret felt trapped by their knowledge. She felt nervous whenever she asked them to do something. Afraid they might turn on her.

"If you don't let us watch this program we'll tell Dad about the sausage."

"If you make us eat this stuff we'll tell Dad you're going to jail."

Margaret was letting them get away with things. Allowing them privileges that she would normally deny. On Tuesday she let them watch three hours of television. She knew this was not good.

Every day when she got up she promised herself she would tell Charles, and every day there was a good reason not to. But she had to tell him on Wednesday because she had to go to court on Thursday and she was sure that there was going to be a reporter there. The only thing that would be worse than telling

Charles that he was married to a kleptomaniac would be to have him read about it in the paper at breakfast.

"Margaret?" she imagined him saying, in a voice so filled with horror and disbelief that the entire family would stop eating.

"Margaret."

Sometimes she would hear him when she was trying to fall asleep.

She imagined herself walking out of the kitchen, without saying anything. Imagined the children watching her as she went upstairs. Imagined Charles sitting at the table when she came back down carrying a suitcase. She knew she would have to leave. Sometimes in this nightmare, Alison, her oldest child, tried to stop her from walking out the front door. But she always left. She wasn't sure where she was going. Just sure that she had to go.

Margaret didn't think of herself as dishonest. She tried not to lie. She tried not to talk behind other people's backs. She hadn't stolen things as a child. Nor as a teenager. She was horrified, twenty years ago, when her sister had been caught at the university bookstore with a copy of *The Rubaiyat of Omar Khayyam* tucked under her sweater.

"Omar Khayyam," Margaret had said. "How could you steal Omar Khayyam?"

Now she was resentful that nothing had happened to her sister. The bookstore manager, unlike the man in the supermarket, had not called the police.

No one seemed to understand how hard it was to buy groceries for a family of five when three of the five, all under eight, came shopping with you. Her friend Beth said grocery shopping with children had to be approached like a military campaign. Margaret's campaigns always turned into routs. When she left the grocery store she inevitably felt like she was retreating. She tried to remember to keep her cart in the middle of each aisle. But she usually forgot and Becky usually managed to pull something off a shelf. Becky had broken a jar of pickles, upset a pyramid of apples and toppled a display of cookies. The worst moments, however, occurred in the cereal aisle. Margaret tried to avoid the cereal aisle—tried to avoid the unpleasantness that descended on her family when she rolled, jaw screwed tight, by the Coco Puffs and the Fruit Loops. She resented what happened in that aisle, she resented having to be the one who always said "*no.*"

"No," she said wearily, for the third time that Thursday afternoon, "we are not buying Fruit Loops."

"No." she said again. "Put the Fruit Loops back, Jonathan."

Jonathan refused to put the large red box he was clutching back on the grocery shelf.

"We aren't getting Fruit Loops," Margaret said again.

"Don't ask me again to buy Fruit Loops."

Margaret turned and pushed her cart firmly out the end of the aisle and down into the next one without looking back.

"They'll follow me," she said to herself as she rounded the corner, anxiously looking behind her.

When her two older children did catch up, Margaret was standing in the spice section by a broken jar of cinnamon. Becky was crying. Margaret was patting her pockets looking for her daughter's soother. She knew they had brought it with them into the supermarket. Becky must have dropped it. Becky was still crying two aisles later, and when Margaret saw the soothers hanging on the wall by the plastic pants and the teething rings, she took one down, removed it from its plastic packaging, and stuck it in her daughter's mouth. Five minutes later Becky was asleep.

When she took it off the wall Margaret had intended to pay for the soother, but by the time she reached the cash registers she had decided that she wouldn't. It wasn't her fault that her child had started to cry. Why should she have to pay to make her stop? If they asked about it at the cash she would say she had forgotten, that she had intended to pay. If they didn't ask she was taking it with her.

She felt a wave of euphoria as she drove out of the parking lot. She had $187.43 worth of groceries in the back of her car. But it was the soother in her daughter's mouth that was making her feel like this. For the first time in her life she was leaving the grocery store feeling as if she had got her money's worth.

She didn't realize what had happened to her until a

week later when she drove into the grocery store parking lot. As she locked the doors of her car and mar-
shalled her children around her shopping cart,
Margaret realized that she intended to steal something
again. Her heart was beating faster. She was scared. But
she felt alive.

Margaret knew what she was going to take. She was
going to take a jar of Vitamin E Collagen Night Cream.
It would be like a present to herself. Something she
ordinarily wouldn't buy. But when they arrived in the
aisle where the night cream was there was a woman
who wouldn't go away. Margaret couldn't take the
cream if someone was standing beside her. The woman
was reading the backs of all the shampoo bottles. One
after another.
    "You're not reading the instructions?" asked Margaret.
    "No," said the woman ruefully, "the promises."

Five minutes later, finding herself alone in the meat
department, she grabbed a pepperoni sausage without
thinking and stuck it up her sleeve. How was she to
know that she was standing in front of a two-way mirror? How was she to know that two butchers and the
store manager were on the other side of the mirror
watching as she slipped the sausage out of sight? It was
just her luck.

When the man approached her in the parking lot she
knew what he wanted.

"Could I take the kids home first," she asked. "Could I get a babysitter and come back and we could talk about it then?"

The man was holding her by the arm—as if she was going to run. She felt tears running down her cheeks.

"I'm sorry," she said. "I'm sorry." Please, she prayed, please let me go home. Please don't make me deal with this in front of my children.

She saw one of the packing boys standing by the door. What do you expect me to do, she thought, make a break?

"We have to go to the office," she said to Jonathan.

"I'll put these bags in the car," she said to the man.

The pepperoni was still up her sleeve. She didn't know what to do about it. She took it out and handed it to the man.

She told Charles on Wednesday night. She was mortified. More ashamed when telling her husband than she was when talking to the policeman who came to the supermarket office.

"I was caught shoplifting at the supermarket," she said. "I have to go to court. I took a pepperoni sausage."

Her husband looked at her.

His wife. His lovely wife standing in front of him in her nightie. He wanted to ask why she had taken the pepperoni. But he knew that wasn't the right question. He thought, You don't know why you do things like that.

"Everyone does that once in their life," he said. Then

he put his arms around her and held her.

"I never took anything before," said Margaret.

He didn't ask her anything, although it just about killed him.

On Thursday, after court, Margaret met Charles for lunch and she told him everything. About the soother and the cereal aisle and the lady reading the shampoo and what it felt like to have a pepperoni sausage in your armpit.

When she finished she said, "One more thing. I don't do groceries any more. Groceries are your job now."

Charles was about to say, when can I do groceries? But he saw she meant it. Instead he said, "I could go on Saturday mornings."

On Saturday he didn't get out of the house until almost noon. He tried to leave without the kids but Margaret said, "Take the kids."

He was gone for two and a half hours.

Margaret read the paper, washed her hair and called her mother.

When he came home she said, "Put everything on the counter. I'll unpack."

She laughed out loud when she found the box of Fruit Loops.

SKUNKS

t was 4:30 in the morning and Dave was having a nightmare about something that smelled bad. Something that smelled bad enough to wake him up. He sat up in bed. His eyes were stinging and to his surprise the smell was still there. It smelled like...skunk. In fact, it smelled like the skunk was in bed with him. He looked at his wife suspiciously. Then he got out of bed and walked around the house. He checked the doors and windows—they were all closed. He went back to sleep telling himself that the smell would be gone by morning.

It wasn't.

He was wakened three hours later by his seven-year-old son, Sam. Sam was standing by the bed poking him.

"There's a skunk in the house," he said. "It smells disgusting."

Dave pulled on a pair of sweat pants and went downstairs. I don't want to deal with skunks, he thought, on his way to check the garden. Please God. Not skunks. Raccoons, Lord. Or squirrels. Please not skunks.

The dog wouldn't go with him. A bad sign. He walked around the house. On the second pass he found a hole leading under his back porch. This will go away, he said to himself.

The odour, however, was still hovering in the house when he came home that evening. It was almost visible, like a haze.

"I can't stand it," said Sam at dinner. "I think I'm going to barf."

"It'll go away," said Dave, without conviction.

The next morning when he got up he thought, the smell wasn't as bad.

"It's not as bad. Is it?" he said to his wife, Morley. "I think it's going."

"Why would a skunk want to live with us?" asked Morley.

Dave didn't answer.

They both knew that the skunk had moved in.

That afternoon someone told Dave there were no skunks in Newfoundland.

"They could have mine," he said, sourly.

The next morning the skunk sprayed just before Dave left for work.

"I'm going to barf," said Sam, helpfully. "Really. I'm going to barf."

Dave took off his jacket and picked up the Yellow Pages.

Exterminators came right after Expropriation Consultants. Just before Extinguishers.

The first two companies he spoke to offered reassurance but no action.

"Skunks eat mice and rats," said the first man. "Why would you want to get rid of it?"

"They're afraid of owls," said the woman at the second company. "Buy one of those plastic owls. It'll be gone in no time. It works. Really."

Dave had to take the plastic owl down on Thursday. It was attracting pigeons. The skunk was still spraying.

He went back to the Yellow Pages and studied the ads more carefully. He was able to group the exterminators into two categories. The first category had names like *Rent-o-kil* and *Sure-kil.* Their ads promised they would send operators who were bonded, insured and fully trained. They also promised to send them in unmarked cars. Dave had a vision of men in radiation suits moving around his backyard with flame-throwers.

The friendlier group called themselves things like *Critter Ridders.* This group used the word *humane* a lot in their ads. These were the companies that fit Dave's image of himself.

Faced with seven pages of ads, Dave had to base his choice on the quality of the artwork. It was a lesson in phone-book iconography. He settled on a company with a half-page picture of a grinning skunk bursting through a suburban roof. Dave figured the big ad was a measure of the company's prosperity—and therefore reliability. He knew it was a tenuous assumption, but what else could he go on?

"We'll send Eric," said the woman on the phone. "He's our skunk man."

Eric came just before lunch.

"We've got to get rid of this one," said Eric shuffling from one foot to the other. "The reason she's spraying—she's trying to attract a mate. If she has babies down there…" Eric didn't finish the sentence. He was shaking his head back and forth. No doubt about it, he looked concerned.

Dave didn't stop to wonder how Eric knew his skunk was a female. He was too horrified by the notion of a family of skunks living under his kitchen to ask. He was ready to do anything that Eric suggested. He thought maybe Eric would put a hose down the hole. But Eric was no fool. He wasn't going to greet a wet skunk in Dave's backyard. He handed Dave a Have-A-Heart Trap. He explained how it worked. One hundred and fifty dollars for a loan of the trap. Dave could keep it until the skunk was caught. When it was, Dave should call. For thirty-five dollars Eric would come and take the skunk away.

"I'll release her in the country," said Eric.

Dave didn't believe the part about the country. He suspected Eric would release the skunk as soon as he was out of sight. He wondered what it would cost to get him to release her near Snider's Record Store. He didn't ask. He was happy to live with the lie about the country.

He went inside and wrote a cheque for one hundred and fifty dollars.

Eric showed Dave how to bait the trap using peanut butter and an apple.

When he came home from the store that night Dave had caught the neighbour's cat, Melissa.

"How much did you pay for the trap?" asked his wife.

"I'm not sure," said Dave.

The skunk sprayed again that night. The smell settled in the house like an unwanted relative.

Tuesday Dave came home and found he had caught a squirrel.

While he was standing in his yard looking at the caged squirrel, Morley phoned Eric.

"No problem," said Eric. "I'll come over and pick her up. I'll release her in the country. Thirty-five dollars."

Morley said Dave would release the squirrel.

"He wanted thirty-five dollars," she said.

"Did you know that?"

"You were here when he came?"

They were more statements of fact than questions.

"You let him do this?"

Dave played dumb.

It was a poor defence but it was the best he could do.

Eric arrived on Wednesday morning unannounced and suggested they move the trap.

"We'll put it right over the hole so the skunk has nowhere else to go," he said.

Wednesday night she dug a new exit.

She sprayed twice on Thursday.

At breakfast Dave imagined he could hear the spray dripping from the floorboards under his kitchen.

Dave wasn't feeling so humane any more. He was feeling humiliated. Walking out the front door in the morning the fresh air hit him the way humidity hits you in summer when you walk out of an air-conditioned room. After he had walked ten blocks—gulping the fresh air like a thirsty man—Dave could still smell a lingering odour of skunk. He was convinced the spray had penetrated his pores.

All day he casually asked customers if they smelled skunk.

"I thought I could smell one," he said.

When his friend Don came in, he asked him point blank.

"Don," he said. "Do I smell like a skunk?"

He wanted to call the men with the flame-throwers and the radiation suits. Morley said, "Let's wait a few more days."

On Friday someone at the store suggested Dave call the Humane Society. It had never occurred to him. He got a recording, a woman's voice:

*Thank you for calling the Humane Society
Wildlife Information line.
For information on: raccoons and squirrels press one,
birds press two,
skunks and foxes press three.*

Dave pressed three.

*Thank you for calling the information line
for skunks and foxes. For information on:
foxes on your property press one,
skunks in your garden press two,
skunks living on your property press three.*

Dave pressed three.

*Thank you for calling the information line for skunks
on your property. If you spot a skunk on your property
gather the following equipment and supplies:
a spotlight, not a flashlight which is not bright enough,
a portable radio, a rag soaked in ammonia or mothballs or
cayenne pepper, a plastic grocery bag with holes
poked into it, a ladder, masking tape, a newspaper
and a broom handle...*

The Humane Society wanted Dave to lower the spotlight, the radio and the ammonia-soaked rag into the skunk hole. The radio, they noted, should be turned on and tuned to a talk station. Not music. Skunks hate talk radio. CBC, thought Dave.

After he had lowered the radio, the rag and the spotlight into the hole, Dave was supposed to tape a single sheet of newspaper over it.

If the skunk wanted in or out she could break through the paper. If she did, break through, Dave was supposed to cover the hole again. If forty-eight hours passed without the paper ripping he could assume the skunk had gone. Then he was supposed to deodorize the hole, fill it in and seal it. The Humane Society did not explain how to deodorize a skunk hole.

Dave bought the supplies before he went home. He had trouble finding a transistor radio.

On Saturday morning, feeling like George Bush, Dave assembled everything and took it out to the yard. He was going to flush the skunk out of its hole the same way the Marines had flushed Manuel Noriega out of the Vatican embassy in Panama.

His attack seemed to incite the skunk to new levels of olfactory offence. For three mornings he carefully replaced the newspaper that the skunk had indignantly broken through.

"What if she is a slow learner?" he asked his wife that night. "What if it's a mentally retarded skunk? What if it's too stupid to leave?"

On the fourth morning the paper was intact. But the odour hanging in the kitchen was just as noxious. At supper Dave found the skunk had dug a new back door and the milk of human kindness left him. If he could have got his hands on the skunk he would have skinned her and nailed her pelt to his front porch.

Dave pulled up the radio and changed the station. This time, on his wife's advice, he tuned it to the all-sports channel. He bought a mister and—rabies be damned—shoved his arm down the skunk hole and sprayed it with ammonia as far as he could reach. Then he emptied a can of red pepper down the hole. He was looking for something that smelled worse than a skunk.

Dave says he thinks the skunk left two days later. Morley says that it was the radio—she says even a skunk can't listen to those jerks for more than a day.

Dave says every time it rains they still smell her. But he is sure the odour is fading. He still has Eric's trap. Has it on the counter at the store. Dave says if he can't sell the trap he'll lend it to anyone who wants it. He says it'll only take a minute to teach them how to set and bait it. He figures Eric knows better than to try and come and pick it up.

SPORTS INJURIES

n Tuesday at lunch Mr. Lanken said, "Jeff, can I see you?" Mr. Lanken was the grade nine math teacher. He was a soft man with a dry sense of humour wasted on teenagers. He smoked Belvedere cigarettes. He was said to be able to smoke an entire cigarette down to the filter with three drags. If his class was good he read a chapter of Conan Doyle to them at the end of every day. He was well liked and a little feared.

Mr. Lanken was also coach of the senior hockey team. Under his guidance the team had won the city championship four of the last ten years. It was a record he was proud of. Mr. Lanken liked coaching.

The hockey team practised two afternoons a week. Their first game was two weeks away. Jeff played left wing.

Jeff did not know why Mr. Lanken wanted to speak to him. He wondered if he was in trouble, but he couldn't imagine why. Maybe Mr. Lanken wanted to move him to defence. Jeff didn't want to play defence. He wanted to play left wing. Maybe Mr. Lanken was going to ask him to be assistant captain. Everyone knew that Steve Langman was going to be captain. Maybe he, Jeff, was going to be an assistant.

Mr. Lanken's desk was in the corner of his classroom on a platform. It was higher than every other desk in the room. When Jeff walked into the room Mr. Lanken was sitting at his desk fiddling with a ruler. There was something about the way Mr. Lanken wouldn't look at him that made Jeff uneasy.

"Come in," said Mr. Lanken. "Sit down. Maybe you should shut the door."

Mr. Lanken was pointing at one of the desks at the front of the classroom.

This moment, this thing that is about to happen, Jeff will remember for the rest of his life. Remember stopping halfway across the room, and going back to close the door, bumping into the desk in the corner, bending down and picking up the books that fell, sitting in the seat below Mr. Lanken's desk. Listening. Tears filling his eyes.

"This is the hardest thing a coach has to do," Mr. Lanken is saying.

Jeff is being cut. Jeff keeps thinking, How am I going to tell my father.

Years later when he tries to describe this moment to his wife, Jeff will say it was like being in a doctor's office. Like he told you you were going to die. Or something. Something like that. You just don't believe it. It all seems unreal.

Mr. Lanken is asking Jeff to be the team manager. He could come to all the games. He could sit on the bench with the players. He could look after the water bottles. Keep the statistics. Help if someone was hurt.

Things like that.

Jeff said, "I'll think about it."

There are ten minutes left in lunch break. He walks to the far end of the football field and stands behind a tree and cries.

⊠ ⊠ ⊠

This is what Jeff Watson knows about his father. He knows his name is Doug. He knows he is fifty-one years old. Maybe fifty-two. Knows he is an engineer—works at the Rayon plant on Cummer Street. Jeff is not exactly sure what he does. Except in the summer he plays golf on the weekends. And in the winter he plays old-timer hockey. Last year Jeff's father went to Las Vegas with guys from his hockey team. It was the second time they went. They stayed for three days. He was married once before but there were no kids. He drives a grey Chrysler Magic wagon. He has a moustache. Lately his hair has been thinning on top. This worries Jeff because someone told him baldness is hereditary and for the last few years whenever Jeff shampoos there is a ball of hair at the bottom of the tub. He knows his father wants new golf shoes for his birthday. He knows he is a Montreal Canadiens fan. And he knows if it wasn't for his knee he could have played in the NHL.

Jeff has heard his father's hockey stories so often that he barely notices the details any more. What he hears are the subtle changes in emphasis—the way a phrase is fine-tuned to fit the occasion. The way the same event can be told with boastful pride one day and wistful regret another. Jeff knows the history by heart, knows that Doug Watson made it as far as Junior A Hockey and no farther. He played centre for the Cornwall Royals. When he was sixteen years old his hero was Emile Descarie. Descarie was a few years older than Doug—already playing in the American Hockey League—one step below the NHL. The year before Doug moved up to junior, Descarie set the record for the most points ever scored in professional hockey in a single season. One hundred and seventy-four points in one year. More than anyone else, anywhere, at any time.

"He was Black Hawk property," Doug liked to say. "But he never got called up. He wasn't a good enough skater. We used to watch him and wonder how you could be as good as Emile Descarie and still not make it."

Doug always shook his head when he said that. Then he added the inevitable coda. The advice. The moral. The whole point of Emile Descarie.

"That's why skating is so important. If you want to make it you have to be able to skate."

If Jeff had been playing well Doug would say that, about skating being important, and make it sound like a compliment. Other times he'd say it so it stung.

Doug never got to play with Emile Descarie but he played with Tex McDermott and Skeeter Wighton. And they both made it all the way to the NHL.

Whenever Doug talked about Tex McDermott he would always end up saying, "Tex. He was a real rink rat." Doug would imbue the words *rink rat* with the kind of respect another father might give *Rhodes Scholar* or *Christian.*

"I played with Tex from the time I was eleven years old," Doug would say.

Then he'd add, "This was in the years before everyone had a Zamboni, you understand. In those days when it was time to flood the ice they'd give everyone a plow and you would get in a line and push the shovels around the rink. Tex used to do this all the time.

"When I was playing with him, Tex was just a role player. First year we made junior I was second-line centre and he was fourth-line wing. Then I hurt my knee and went away to college and didn't see him play until the next winter.

"I saw two games that year. The other game I saw, I came down to see Lafleur play. I was not impressed. I played against him once. And I was bigger and stronger and faster than him. But Tex was astounding. I hadn't seen him for a year and he had gone from being a marginal player to being a star. On one play he wound up behind the Royal's net and got to the blue line and then he pushed the puck forward—just a little push—and he caught up to it at the centre line and slapped the puck and beat the goalie cleanly—before he even had a chance to move. I'll never forget that. It's amazing when you see a guy score from centre ice. He was drafted by Philadelphia. The same year they drafted Bobby

Clarke. They chose Tex ahead of Bobby. Everyone said Clarke *might* make it—but Tex, everyone thought that Tex was a shoe in."

The other guy that Jeff knew all about was Skeeter Wighton. Skeeter played nets for the Boston Bruins. But Skeeter's father played the most important role in Doug Watson's parables. Doug would turn to Skeeter's dad whenever he was building up to something important.

"Skeeter's father used to drive him crazy. Every time we went to his place his father would start up, 'Let's play ball hockey. Do you guys want to play ball hockey?' Skeeter would roll his eyes and say, We're going out.

"After the games parents weren't allowed in the dressing room but they'd all be hanging around outside the door. Skeeter's father would be right at the front of the crowd and as soon as Skeeter came out he'd start lecturing him about the game and what he'd done wrong—it was always what he'd done wrong. Sometimes they would drive me home and his father would keep going on about it and Skeeter would sit in the back seat giving him the finger. Skeeter was supposed to practise shooting the puck half an hour every day in the backyard. His father would come home at supper and say, You done your shooting yet? Skeeter quit after our first year of midget. He said he couldn't stand it any more. Said it wasn't him out there skating. It was his dad. He had no sense of individuality."

Then Doug would say, "That's why I don't tell you what to do unless you ask me."

That was Jeff's cue. When Doug said that Jeff was supposed to ask if there was something about his game Doug had noticed. Was there something he wanted to tell him? If he didn't ask, Doug would tie himself into knots and tell him anyway, so Jeff had learned when his father started talking about Skeeter Wighton's dad it was best to ask for advice as quick as possible and get it over with.

Skeeter didn't play hockey for four years. He started playing again in college. But he went in nets. Which was the only position his father had never played. He made the Olympic team and was drafted by the Bruins after the '72 games.

"He was a natural," said Doug. "A real natural."

Jeff always assumed that the point of this story was that Skeeter Wighton might be able to get away with that sort of thing but that he, Jeff, who they both knew was not a *natural*, would have to *practise* if he wanted to get anywhere.

Doug went to all of Jeff's games and most of the practices. He always sat by himself. He didn't like to socialize with the other parents. He'd sit there and drink coffee and watch everything carefully. Sometimes visiting teams thought he was a scout.

After one game last year, when Jeff had been cross-checked into the boards in the second period, Doug took him out to dinner. As they were sitting in their booth looking at the menus Doug said, "You should have hit that kid."

They were at the Swiss Chalet.

Doug said, "When I was in junior I lost the first fifteen fights I was in. But it was necessary to keep fighting. If it looked like I was going to back down they would have been all over me."

Jeff thought, so that's why we came here. Then he said, "It was Andy Bailey who hit me. Andy is my friend."

Doug said, "You know what my father taught me? He taught me that there are no friends in hockey. And he was right. I had to beat up a lot of my friends. I'm not proud of that but it's what I had to do."

Doug leaned back and flashed a big grin at the waitress who was standing there waiting to take their order.

As he watched his father order it occurred to Jeff that his father *was* proud of it. He *was* proud of beating his friends up.

"Before every game I prepared myself not to have friends on the ice. I took on a totally different character when I was playing. I would sit in the dressing room and turn myself into a different person. I would think about the team we were going to play and I would feel numb. I feel it now sort of."

Jeff couldn't believe this was happening in a restaurant.

Doug said, "If you hit me now I probably wouldn't feel it."

Jeff glanced at the nearby tables. He didn't want to

do this here.

"Not in the face," said Doug. "But anywhere else."

Jeff shook his head. No. Not here.

Doug said, "I had to get like that because when I went on the ice I had to be ready to give and receive. So I got this numbness."

Jeff was still shaking his head. He said, "I'd never fight Andy Bailey. Andy Bailey is my friend."

When the chicken came they ate in silence. When he had finished Doug asked for a second roll. He used it to mop up the sauce left on his plate. Then he began to tell the Boston story. It went like this.

Once Doug was playing in a tournament in Boston and he had been billeted with the family of one of the kids he was playing against. The kid was the goalie and in the second game of the tournament he had wandered out of the crease and Doug had hit him so hard that the kid had to be carried off the ice. After the game when Doug got back to the house, his bags were packed and waiting on the porch. He knew it wasn't an invitation to ring the door bell. So he picked up his bags and went to a pay phone and called his coach. The coach tried to get another family to take him in but no one would have him. They all knew who he was and what he had done. They had to get him a hotel room instead.

The waitress came and asked if they wanted dessert. They both ordered a caramel sundae. As the waitress was walking away, Doug called her back and asked for extra caramel. The waitress looked at Jeff. He shook his head, no.

But Doug said, "Go on." Then turned to the waitress and said, "He'll have extra too."

Then he said, "I had this little radio. It was just a cheap transistor for the bus and they forgot to pack it. I figured it was gone for good. It came in the mail two weeks later. I thought that was classy. That they'd take the time to send it like that. It showed that they had no hard feelings. They could have thrown it out."

It was the first time Jeff had heard the radio part before.

He perked up.

He said, "You still got the radio?"

⊠ ⊠ ⊠

Most of Doug's stories *were* true. It was true, for instance, he *had* played with Tex McDermott and Skeeter Wighton. And it was true that both Skeeter and Tex went on to play in the NHL. But it wasn't the whole truth. Tex only played eight games for Philadelphia before he was sent down and he never made it back. He only weighed 160 pounds the year he was drafted and when the Philly coaches saw him they said, "You should put on some weight," and they put him on supplements and a weight-lifting program. He gained forty or fifty pounds that summer and in the fall he couldn't play hockey any more. There was no explanation for it but Doug suspected it wasn't the weight. He figured that all those years pushing the shovel around and around the Cornwall arena had given Tex a long powerful stride. He had great speed if he had room to get going, but he wasn't quick. In the NHL no one gave Tex the space he needed to pick up speed. Last time Doug saw him, Tex was a drug addict. Doug never told Jeff that part of the story.

And he didn't tell him everything that happened to Skeeter Wighton either. How he was in nets against the Leafs the night Darryl Sittler had his ten-point game. Six goals and four assists. The final score: Toronto eleven, Boston four. In between the second and third period Skeeter asked to be taken out of the game and one of his defencemen looked at him and said, "Fuck you, sieve-head."

The time Skeeter told Doug about that game he said that when he skated onto the ice for the third period he had a vision of Eddie Shore. Shore used to make his goaltenders practise with a belt fastened around their necks, tied to the crossbar of the net. Skeeter said every time Sittler got on the ice he could feel the belt choking him. Then he said Sittler was laughing whenever he got near the net.

"He was fucking laughing," he said. "The prick. I lost my concentration. Fuck."

It wasn't all Skeeter lost. After the game Skeeter walked out of the dressing room and took a taxi to the airport and got a plane home. He hadn't played hockey since. Doug hadn't told Jeff that part.

It was also true that Doug had played against Guy

Lafleur. And it was true that when they played against each other Doug *was* bigger, and stronger and faster than Lafleur. What he neglected to tell his son, however, was that Doug was twelve years old at the time they played and Lafleur was only ten—playing a division up.

Doug didn't think of these as lies. He just didn't see the point of telling his son the bad stuff. What good would that do? What he knew was a lie, however, was that he had been kept out of the NHL by a bum knee. That wasn't true. The truth was that Doug never got big enough to play professional hockey. He might have been bigger than Guy Lafleur when he was twelve years old but by the time he was sixteen Guy Lafleur and just about everybody else was bigger than Doug. When he was eighteen and still only 5'7", 145 pounds, Doug could see the writing on the wall.

Hockey, unlike baseball, is not a sport that lends itself to statistics. But most hockey fans know a few of the games' numbers—the goals scored by their favourite player last season, say, or the number of minutes in penalties someone has served. Doug specialized in heights. When he was eighteen he knew the height of everyone in the League. Bobby Hull was 5'10". Stan Mikita was 5'9". Henri Richard was 5'7"—so was Yvan Cournoyer—but there were darn few of them.

That summer, the summer he was eighteen, someone told Doug you could stretch out your spine and add an inch or so to your height by hanging from a bar. Doug got a harness from a sailing school and rigged it up so he could swing from the rod in his closet. The summer he was eighteen he used to dangle in there like a bat for an hour every night and when he got down he actually was a half an inch taller. But it didn't last.

He tried everything. He read where Rosey Grier, a three-hundred-pound football player, had put on weight with Metrical. Everyone else was drinking it to lose weight but Rosey drank three glasses before each meal. Doug tried to do that too, but he couldn't keep it up and he didn't put on any weight to speak of.

Years later he read the story of the Japanese guy who wanted to make the police force and was caught banging himself on the head with a mallet. The guy was trying to create a callous on the top of his head that would give him an extra inch or two. Doug understood completely.

What he didn't understand was what happened the autumn he was nineteen. He went to training camp thinking he had made the Royals—he had played for them the last two years—but he got cut after two weeks. He couldn't believe it. There were a couple of rough days after that. There was some anger. There was a sense that they were wrong. But there was a sense that they were right too.

The next day Doug went out for the football team. Two weeks later he blew his knee and that was the end of that. Four years later he was watching a hockey game on TV with his first wife and Skeeter Wighton was playing and he said, "I used to play with that guy."

Then he said that he did his knee playing hockey and that's why he hadn't made the NHL with Skeeter and Tex.

"Otherwise I would have been there," he said. "And we never would have met."

That was the first time he told the story and even while he was telling her he wondered why he was doing it. But over the years he had stuck with it—all the time adding little embellishments—how he had caught a blade going behind the net—how he skated off the ice and collapsed behind the bench, how he had a contract with Detroit but there was an escape clause if he was injured. How they hadn't paid him anything. Bastards.

If he had still been living in Cornwall he couldn't have got away with the story—but they were living halfway across the country. He never saw any of those guys any more.

■ ■ ■

Jeff didn't have to tell his father he had been cut. His mother did that for him.

She called just as Doug was leaving his office to go down into the plant.

"I've only got a minute," he said.

Then she told him and he said, "He must have been fooling around. He was being a jerk. Why else would they cut him? He was doing something stupid on the ice. Or something."

Then Rosemary said something that took his breath away. "Maybe," she said, "he wasn't good enough."

Always before, when her son was hurt, Rosemary Watson knew how to comfort him. A hug used to help. But this time it wasn't his knee that was scraped—it was his dignity. What Jeff wanted, and what Rosemary found so hard to accept, was to be left alone. She felt angry.

"If you hadn't made such a big deal about hockey," she said to Doug on the phone, "this wouldn't have happened. He's upstairs. I walked by his room. I heard him crying. I hate this."

Doug said, "If you had let him go to hockey camp he would have made it."

Rosemary said, "He did go to hockey camp."

Doug said, "For two weeks. I mean all summer."

Rosemary hung up without saying goodbye. Just hung up. Click.

Doug swore at the phone.

Shit.

⌧   ⌧   ⌧

Doug was confused. He didn't care if Jeff made the team or not. He did care. He wanted him to make the team. But he only wanted him to make the team for his own sake. Because *he* wanted to. Because it would be fun. He never wanted him to play professional hockey. He wanted him to play professional hockey. Longed to be able to go to a game in the Gardens and watch his son. Visit the dressing room after the game.

That night, the night Jeff was cut, Doug went upstairs and knocked on his son's bedroom door, went in, turned the stereo down and sat on the edge of the bed. Said, "I know how bad you must feel but…"

Jeff said, "You have no idea how I feel. *You* were never cut."

Jeff felt guilty for letting his father down. He felt embarrassed in front of his friends at school who had made the team. He felt ashamed to be asked to be the manager. The water boy.

* * *

Doug went downstairs and drank a beer. Found Rosemary watching television. Waited for a commercial. Said, "If I tell you something do you promise you'll never tell anyone ever. Ever?"

Rosemary felt a horrible whirling in her stomach. She looked at her husband and thought, I don't want to know this. He's having an affair. Why can't he keep it to himself?

She nodded her head, yes. I promise.

Her heart was pounding.

He told her the about his knee. About being too small to play hockey. About getting cut.

"What should I do?" he asked. "Should I tell him?"

"What do you think you should do?" she said.

STUART McLEAN

Doug said, "I'll tell him tomorrow."

※ ※ ※

Doug came home from work and said, "I can't stop thinking about Mr. Reynolds."

Rosemary said, "Who?"

Doug said, "Mr. Reynolds. The coach who cut me. We called him Allie. His real name was Roger. Allie was his nickname. I never understood why until this week."

"Why what?"

"Why we called him Allie."

"Why?"

"There was a pitcher for the New York Yankees called Allie Reynolds. He died this week."

"The baseball player or your coach?"

"The baseball player. He won the World Series for New York over the Brooklyn Dodgers in 1952 at Ebbets Field. You know what it said about him in the newspaper?"

"What?"

"They interviewed his grandson. He said Allie was still throwing pitches in the hospital. In his sleep. Right up to before he died. He said he would put his hands together and he'd rough up the leather and he'd hurl his arm back and throw."

"What did he die of?"

"Cancer."

"But still dreaming of baseball."

161

"Yeah. I'm going to tell him tonight."

◼ ◼ ◼

Doug didn't tell him that night. Or the next one.

Said, "I thought about it. Telling him would be worse."

Rosemary said, "OK."

Doug said, "You think I failed him don't you?"

Rosemary said, "We all find a way to fail our kids."

Doug said, "Yeah, but…"

Rosemary said, "But nothing. You're never going to be any good as a father until you accept the fact that you are going to screw it up. Once you accept that you'll do fine."

She was taking off her earrings, attaching one to the other so they wouldn't get separated, dropping them into the little box on her bureau.

"You still think I should tell him the truth."

"That's up to you. The truth usually works pretty good. It's not important any more. It's probably too late anyway."

◼ ◼ ◼

The night he was cut, the night his father came upstairs and tried to talk to him, Jeff lay on his bed for an hour listening to tapes before he got up and began aimlessly tidying his room. He hadn't cried like that for years. He was surprised how tired and light he felt. He doesn't know what has happened but he knows he is not going to hear his father's hockey stories again soon. He knows that some division, some difference has come between them. He wanders across his room to the bulletin board above his desk and pulls down the hockey schedule that is pinned there. He crumples it into a tight ball and throws it across the room. The ball of paper arcs towards the garbage can, hits the rim and bounces onto the floor. Jeff smiles as he picks it up, stands back, lifts his arm, takes another shot.

SHIRTS

he first shirt to disappear was a Hathaway—a bold blue-striped shirt with a formal white collar. It was the shirt Dave was married in. He noticed it was missing one Saturday evening when he was dressing to go out.

"Morley," he called, to his wife. "I can't find my wedding shirt."

The Hathaway was not the sort of shirt Dave normally bought for himself. He thought it was flamboyant, and he felt self-conscious whenever he wore it. But he was proud of owning it. And proud he had worn it the afternoon he got married.

He had been gloriously drunk the day he bought it. The salesman, an enthusiastic young man in an oversized sweater and floppy black pants, kept pouring him shot glasses of a licorice-tasting liquor. Nothing like that had ever happened to Dave before. He usually shopped at Eaton's. He had already bought a shirt at Eaton's that he was planning to wear at his wedding—a white one. He wandered into the men's store looking for a tie to go with the white shirt.

He was looking at a rack of muted striped ties when the salesman breezed up to him.

"I'm getting married," said Dave. "I need a tie."

"This is a happy event?" asked the salesman.

Dave nodded dumbly.

"Those aren't wedding ties," said the salesman, waving his hand disdainfully. "Those are funeral ties."

Dave followed the salesman across the store, obediently.

They stopped in front of a display of the most colourful ties Dave had ever seen. The salesman flicked two of them off the rack and said, "These are wedding ties."

The ties were so exuberant Dave actually took a step backwards.

"This *is* a happy occasion?" asked the salesman again. "You are *happy* about this marriage?"

"Yes," said Dave. "But…"

That's when the salesman took Dave over to the cash register and poured him his first drink.

"Yes, but what?" asked the salesman.

Dave didn't know "but what?"

The only "but" he knew was that he had never worn a tie so…so…

"Happy," said the salesman. "It's a happy tie."

The salesman poured him another drink.

Dave threw it back.

Eventually he said, "OK… I'll take the red one."

The salesman smiled.

"Good," he said. "Now. About the white shirt."

After two more shots of liquor Dave blew out of the store with the bright red tie and the blue-striped shirt with the white collar.

Dave spent some time with the shirt every day during the three weeks before his wedding. Mostly he took it out of its box and laid it on his bed and arranged the tie on top of it and stared at them. Sometimes he stared for five or ten minutes. He had never owned anything like these things in his life. They made him feel reckless. He showed them to his friends and asked, "Do you think they're OK? Can I wear them when I get married?" His friends said yes, yes they were fine.

He didn't wear the shirt or the tie often after he was married but he liked having them in his cupboard. Just having them there made him feel dashing.

Morley said, no. No, she hadn't seen his wedding shirt.

He wondered if he had taken it to a dry-cleaner and forgotten to pick it up. He used to drop his shirts at a number of places and it was possible he had taken the wedding shirt somewhere and forgotten about it. He visited every dry-cleaner he had ever gone to. He said, "I've lost my ticket."

It was a lie but he thought if he was tentative about the missing shirt they wouldn't look as hard as they would if he claimed they had it. Nothing turned up.

There was another possibility.

Morley had thrown his shirt out.

The more Dave thought about it the more he seemed to remember putting the shirt in a green garbage bag with a pile of other clothes he wanted to take to the cleaners. Morley must have mistaken the bag for garbage.

Dave was predisposed to believe his wife might have done this. His mother had thrown out so much of his stuff over the years. Why would his wife be any different? His baseball cards were gone, his cowboy guns, his leather holster, his comic-book collection, and most incredibly, his table-hockey game. "You are forty years old," his mother said, the day he asked where his hockey game was. "You threw it out," he said. She couldn't understand his incredulity, his anger. She might as well have thrown out his childhood. In his memory he had spent years playing table-hockey. If there was no one to play with he would prepare the ice—pushing a wet lump of Kleenex around the game—imagining he was driving a Zamboni. If his mother could throw out his hockey game, why couldn't his wife throw out the shirt he was married in?

The wedding shirt had been missing long enough that it had become something Morley and Dave could laugh about. So when Dave said, "Where's my plaid shirt? The green and brown one."

Morley said, "I threw it out."

Dave understood this was supposed to be a joke.

Dave had bought the plaid shirt near Kennebunk, Maine. He bought it on the last day of their summer vacation, at a factory outlet. It was a wonderful shirt—green with brown checks. It was a shirt that fit Dave's image of himself—casual, but dressy at the same time.

A shirt you could wear a woven tie with. The way writers do. Or university professors—or, more to the point, the way Robert Redford did in *All The President's Men*. It was a perfect shirt—and it was all the more perfect because it was blessed by so many happy associations. It reminded Dave of the ocean. Of the ice-cream truck that whistled up to the beach every afternoon.

A week after it went missing Morley said, "I think I washed that shirt last weekend. I think I remember hanging it on the line. I can't remember taking it down."

"Someone stole it," said Dave. "Someone came into the yard and stole my shirt."

Dave was so fond of the plaid shirt that this seemed reasonable.

"It was Gavin," he said. "The bastard."

Gavin lives two houses away from Dave and Morley. He is a writer. He works at home.

"Writers never have any money," said Dave. "He had motive and he had opportunity. He's home all day. It would be easy for Gavin to sneak into our yard and swipe my shirt."

The green and brown checked shirt went missing in the fall.

It turned up the following spring.

It literally walked through the front door—on Jim Scoffield's back. Dave and Morley had invited Jim to dinner.

He turned up in Dave's missing plaid shirt.

Jim Scoffield lives on the corner. He is a fifty-two-year-old bachelor. He is also an artist and a great favourite in the neighbourhood. He is from the Maritimes and committed to the spirit of neighbourhood. He spends more time than necessary on his front lawn—poking at plants—not so much gardening as gabbing with the river of neighbours as they flow up and down the street on their way past his house to the arena or the library. In a large sense Jim *is* the neighbourhood—and whenever he starts talking about moving back to Nova Scotia people get worried. Being a bachelor Jim never entertains, except when he is invited to someone's house for dinner, which happens often, and then he is always entertaining. It is not unusual for someone to look at a large stew on the stove and say, "We can't eat all that. Why don't we call Jim?"

Dave likes Jim because Jim lived in Toronto during the 1960s. He lived on Lowther Avenue across from Joni Mitchell. Dave loves to hear stories about the parties, about the top floor bedroom in Jim's rooming house—about goings on at The Riverboat.

So Dave couldn't believe it when Jim wore his shirt to dinner.

"That was unbelievable," he said after supper. "It was unbelievable."

Dave was pacing back and forth as if he had just witnessed a murder.

"Calm down," said Morley, unhelpfully.

"Calm down? Our neighbour—my friend—walked into our house wearing a shirt he stole from our clothesline," said Dave.

"Maybe he owns the same shirt," said Morley.

"Unlikely," said Dave.

"Maybe he found it. Maybe it blew off the line and he found it on his lawn."

"Come on," said Dave. "He stole the shirt from our line."

"If he stole the shirt," said Morley, "why would he wear it here to dinner?"

"Because he has forgotten. Consciously. Subconsciously he feels guilty about taking it. He wants to return it. Wearing it to dinner tonight was like…it was like a confession. His subconscious compelled him to bring it back—to show us what he had done."

"Why don't you ask him?" said Morley

"Are you crazy? What if he did take it? What's he going to say. 'Yeah, I took the shirt.' Do you think he's going to admit to stealing a shirt off our line?"

That night as they went to bed, Dave said, "You know how they talk about murderers? 'He was so nice. He was a quiet guy. We can't believe he did it.'"

"Yes?" said Morley.

"Maybe Jim is like that. Maybe he *is* crazy. Maybe he wore the shirt into our house on purpose. Maybe he's playing with us."

Morley was almost asleep. Dave was sitting up in bed as if he was driving a semi-trailer across the continent—

his eyes burning across the bedroom.

"Dave?"

"What."

"You have to talk to him."

"Think of what you are saying." Dave was waving his hands around the bedroom. "Think of the repercussions. If he took the shirt—and I ask him about it—it's the end of our friendship. He's our neighbour. I like him. I really like him. Even if he did take the shirt, I still like him. Maybe he has some weird thing about stealing clothes. I can live with that. I want to stay friends more than I want the shirt back."

"We'll never know," said Morley.

"Right," said Dave. "We'll never know."

Whenever you take a stand like that—a stand based on principles—you can be certain your principles will be put to the test. Dave's test came on a Saturday afternoon the next April. It was a glorious afternoon. What snow remained was melting into the gardens. The sun was shining. The sky was blue. The air was warm on your face. It was good enough just to be alive. Morley was gardening. Dave was carrying things for her.

"This is so wonderful," she said. She was down on her knees pulling the mulch out of her garden.

"You pull all the dead stuff up and there's life pumping away underneath it."

She took Dave on a tour of her garden.

"Those are snowdrops," she said. "These are daffodils coming. These are tulips."

STUART M^CLEAN

She pulled up a handful of dead leaves.

"Pretty soon we're going to be dead stuff, too," she said.

The thought seemed to please her.

Dave put his arm around his wife and thought how lucky he was to have married her. Then he looked up and saw Jim coming down the street carrying a bag of laundry. Jim was limping.

"My knee," he said.

"Give me the money," said Dave. "I'll take it down and put it in."

Jim gave him a handful of quarters and the bag of laundry.

The laundromat is at the bottom of the street.

Dave said, "I'll be back in a minute."

When he came back Jim was gone. Morley was back on her knees.

"It's there," he said

"What's there?" asked Morley.

"The shirt is there. My shirt is there. And it *is* mine. I actually put *my* shirt into the washing for *him*."

Dave had a plan.

"I'm going to steal it back," he said. "And then you know what I am going to do? I am going to wear it over to his house."

Morley said, "Why don't you just ask him about the shirt."

"This is much better," said Dave, running inside.

That night at supper Morley said, "You didn't do it."

175

"No," said Dave. "I didn't do it. I wanted to, but I couldn't. I either like him too much or I am too much of a coward. What if he really is crazy? It's not worth it."

All summer whenever Dave saw Jim wearing his brown and green plaid shirt, he would feel his stomach knot.

One day he came home and said, "He's got paint on it, damn it."

"Why don't you just say 'nice shirt' and see what he says?" said Morley.

"You don't understand," said Dave. "If I say anything about the shirt he'll know."

One Saturday in September Dave took Sam to the library. On their way home they stopped to talk to Jim.

Jim has a rail fence. The kind you might see at a horse farm. A fence made for kids to climb—for adults to lean on. So while Dave and Jim leaned against the fence, Sam played.

"Look," said Sam, after five, maybe ten minutes.

"Look," he said, pulling at Dave's pants. "Look what I found."

He was holding a pair of glasses.

"I found them," he said, pointing at the sidewalk. "I found them by the tree."

Dave looked at Jim.

"They're not mine," said Jim.

Sam wanted to keep the glasses.

"They're not ours," said Dave. "We should take them home and make a sign in case someone is looking for them. You can make the sign, Sam."

"You could put them on the fence," said Jim. "Someone might find them if you leave them there."

And then Jim said, "I've found the strangest things on the fence over the years."

And then he said, "Two years ago I found a shirt. Right on the sidewalk. Right there."

He was pointing at the sidewalk where Dave often parked his car.

And then he said, "I figured someone was taking the shirt to the cleaners and they dropped it getting out of their car so I put it over the fence and left it there for a few days. I figured the guy who owned it would probably come back and find it. No one did. I have been wearing it for two years. It's a great shirt."

"A green one," said Dave. "With brown checks."

"Yeah," said Jim. "Did I tell you this already?"

It turned out that Jim had kept the shirt in his house for six months before he had the courage to wear it outside.

"I was afraid someone would recognize it," he said. "The first time I wore it was the night I came to your place for dinner. Do you remember that night? It's a great shirt."

Dave invited Jim for supper again. Jim went home and changed into the shirt. He bought two bottles of wine, but he didn't offer to give the shirt back.

"Hell no. It's mine now," he said, when Dave finally asked.

Dave felt buoyant. Only a friend would say that.

"I should have taken it back," said Dave to Morley when they went to bed. "That afternoon at the laundromat. I should have stolen it. It would have made a better ending."

THE SECRET OF LIFE

Spring was colder and wetter than it had been for years. So much rain fell in April that it was impossible to get a tractor into the fields. The rain kept falling into May and with each grey morning Mike Vandenberg became increasingly agitated. All he could do was pace around his property, scowling at the sky, the livestock, his wife.

On the second Monday of the month he butchered a chicken without being asked. As she watched from the kitchen it occurred to Claire that her husband was getting more pleasure than he should from the execution. It did not surprise her. Early in their marriage Claire Vandenberg learned to gauge her husband's state of mind by the number of chicken carcasses in the freezer. On Tuesday Mike killed two more even though the first one was still in the fridge. Two days later, when the weather still hadn't cleared, he appeared on the porch looking like a surgeon who had run amok, handed Claire four dead birds and left without a word.

On Friday after school Claire drove her son into town. He had an appointment with the orthodontist to have his bands removed. When he had finished at the dentist Sean got into the car and tugged the rear-view mirror around so he could admire his mouth. Claire was about to say; *Don't, I need the mirror.* But she thought, He needs it more than I do. So she didn't say anything.

Sean said, "It's so weird to feel my teeth with my tongue. They're so smooth. Can I get some gum? I never thought they'd be off."

The surprise at home was that the change in Sean's behaviour was even more dramatic than the change in his appearance. Before supper he sat at the kitchen table and talked with his mother while she cooked. When the meal was finished he helped with the dishes. Claire wondered if Dr. Miller might have had the bands on too tight.

The bands hadn't come off a moment too soon. Plans were well under way at the high school for the graduation dance. The theme was: A Night in Paris. The dance committee was building a cardboard Eiffel Tower which they were going to erect in the middle of the cafeteria. After last year's fiasco Mr. Kenton has been overseeing the construction. Last year's dance, A Night in Cairo, went off the rails when Mr. O'Neil, the English teacher and last year's chaperone, discovered that the committee had hauled three mattresses down from the infirmary and arranged them inside the huge brown paper pyramid they had built against the north wall. "No enclosed spaces" was this year's rule, which explained Mr. Kenton's satisfaction with the essentially see-through Eiffel Tower.

Sean still didn't have a date for the dance. He was planning to phone Allison Blackburn after supper. He had called once already but had hung up when Allison's mother answered.

Usually when he wanted to ask a girl out Sean went to the phone booth at the 7-Eleven so no one could overhear him. Asking a girl out, like confession, was not something he wanted to share with his family.

Calling Allison was going to be the second hard thing that Sean did that week. Earlier he had told his father that he had been accepted by Bishop's University, and that he wanted to go to school in the Eastern Townships in the province of Quebec. Sean had kept the acceptance letter hidden for two weeks. But he had to mail his deposit by the end of the month so there was no holding off.

Sean's announcement hung over the dinner table like the rain clouds over the Vandenbergs' fields. Sean felt awful. For the first time in his life he felt afraid for his father. He was convinced that leaving the farm was taking the easy way out.

After dinner Sean helped with milking. Then he went to the 7-Eleven and hung up again when Allison's mother answered the phone. He had to wait for a half-hour before he could phone again. He didn't want the Blackburns to suspect it was him who had been hanging up.

The next morning Sean had a fight with his father about the car. Mike said there was no way anyone was going to take a car to A Night in Paris—especially if they were going to stay up to watch the sun rise on the Lake Road. They finished milking in a steamy silence. Sean was almost late for the bus.

The night of the dance he picked up Allison in the car. But he was in the back seat. Mike was driving. It was a compromise Sean wasn't happy with. He accepted it to avoid the indignity of going to his grade twelve graduation by bike.

For the rest of the summer things were strained between father and son. Sean felt guilty about leaving his father alone on the farm. As sad as Mike was, and he was sad because part of him wished his boy would stay and take over the farm, another part of him was proud of his son. But Sean wouldn't have believed that in a hundred years—even if Mike was able to tell him.

For his part Mike was quieter than usual. He wanted to tell his only son something important before he went to college. It reminded him of the summer he had tried to talk to Sean about sex. He had thought about it for weeks and when he finally felt the right moment had arrived, the things that he had planned to say had been plugged up inside of him for so long that they flew out in one long frantic burst. When he finished Mike said, "Have you got any questions?" Only after he said it did he notice how horrified his son looked.

Sean said, "You're joking."

Mike said, "No, no. It's true."

But Sean didn't want to believe him. He said, "Do we have to talk about this now?"

Mike said, "Oh. OK. Forget it."

Claire said, "Maybe he's still too young."

They had never talked about sex again.

Mike thought he could do better this time if he could only work out what it was he wanted to say. He figured it was his last shot.

The summer spun by faster than ever. For much of August Mike imagined lengthy conversations with his boy. Sometimes he practised on the livestock, telling the cows, twenty years comes up faster than you realize. He considered the hard times in his life. All the things he had been afraid of. All those years wasted, he told himself, because I was terrified of being different. That's why all us fifty-four-year-olds end up looking so much alike. All of us are terrified of being different.

As the weeks jogged towards the first harvest Mike would have to handle without his son, the two seemed to grow testier towards each other. They fought about the car. Mike seemed to resent being asked for it and Sean seemed to resent asking. Mike wondered if that was what happened when you moved away from home...you got too big for your britches. Mostly he wondered what a dairy farmer who had never been near a college could tell a kid who was about to go to one. He was confused and miserable.

⊠ ⊠ ⊠

Sean wasn't feeling much better. He was anxious to begin his life as an adult but he couldn't shake the feeling that all the good times had been used up. His grandfather had got to fight in the last decent war. His father had taken on the farm when farms still counted. What was left for him?

One night he made a list of the things he had missed.

—smoking
—LSD
—anxiety-free sex
—suntanning
—any kind of sex
—even making out with Jenny Moore at the drive-in
—drive-ins
—Woodstock
—Vietnam
—hippies
—bell bottoms
—life before feminism
—Motown
—Led Zeppelin

He could as well have added Janis Joplin, John Lennon, Black Sabbath, The Velvet Underground, the Beatles, The Who and Pink Floyd.

He was eighteen years old.

"Shit," said his friend Bruce one night as they sat on the swings in the schoolyard. "It's eleven o'clock on a Saturday night and we're on the same swings we played on when we were eight. We should be wearing pants too big for us and taking advantage of the Young Offenders Act."

They were supposed to be having the time of their lives, but they both felt their lives were already over. They both had a sinking feeling that no matter how hard they worked in college there wouldn't be jobs for them when they graduated.

Sean was having trouble falling asleep at night. He would toss and turn and then he would get frantic and get up and wash his face and try to calm down and start again. Then he'd start thinking if he didn't get to sleep in ten minutes he would get sick or something awful would happen. He would glance at the clock and see another ten minutes had sped by as he flounced around the bed. Crying. Scared. One night he was so sure that he was going to die in his sleep that he got out of bed and wrote a note to his parents. It said: I love you. I'm sorry.

Bruce talked about going to Paris at the end of the summer. Or what about Vancouver? We could go out west.

Vancouver would be good, said Sean. He knew they weren't going anywhere.

◪ ◪ ◪

Mike settled on what he wanted to say to his son near the end of August. He stood in the barn one afternoon and watched the cows shouldering each other and decided they would talk after milking—in the morning, when the dew was still on the grass. They would stand in the door of the barn and look out at the corn field by the house and he would tell his son that it was a beautiful world and anything in the world was possible. He would tell him that his heart's desire was possible and that he should never waste time looking for permission to do anything. Not from him and not from anyone. Anything he wanted to do he should just do it. He would tell him that he had long ago stopped being surprised by the generosity of people. And that the things that had given him his greatest happiness were his family. His friends. His neighbours. Like the Bible said, Love thy neighbour.

One night Mike thought...he had spent all this time thinking of what *he* wanted to say to his boy and what he really wanted was to have Sean say something to *him*. He ached to hear his son forgive him for his inadequacies as a parent. For the times he had spanked him. For the times he had been impatient. For the times he had been curt. For the time he had kept him home to do chores when everyone else was swimming.

Mike wanted Sean to tell him he had been an OK father.

The morning finally arrived when Mike had decided they would talk. He woke Sean and headed out to the barn. He opened a new grain bag and sprinkled a can of oats in front of the stallion. He relished the sound the horse made as he chased the oats down with a muzzle of water. Mike wished he could make such happy noises as he ate.

They did the milking together as usual. Sean carrying the full containers to the holding tank. Mike moving the milkers from cow to cow, wiping the udders with disinfectant before clamping the suction cups in place. When he got to the last cow he cleared his throat and called his son. Sean looked up to see Mike peering into the milker that he was holding. Perhaps he was nervous. He had been planning the next moment for weeks. He certainly wasn't thinking clearly because, instead of clamping the suction hose onto the last cow, he brought it up to his mouth. It looked like he was blowing a speck of dust or something out of the hose. He must have brought it too close because suddenly the hose seemed to leap forward and attach itself to his lips and he bellowed. It was a muffled sort of bellow. He pawed at the hose with both hands and in a panic realized it wasn't coming off. He felt like his innards were going to be sucked out into the milker. He thought, Is this how I am going to die? A milker? He clamped his teeth closed hoping that this might stop any organs from spilling out of his mouth. Then he staggered to his feet pulling at the hose and roaring at the same time. Instead of reaching out and turning the contraption off, Sean just stared in horror. His father was staggering towards him. He looked like a snake trainer wrestling with an Anaconda. With one final pull Mike ripped the hose off his mouth. He stood shaking and pale in front of his son, sweat pouring from his face, his shirt-tail out.

Sean drove him to hospital. He needed seven stitches in his lower lip.

Sean said he wanted the car to go to the station to buy a train ticket for Bishop's. And Mike said, "Why not just take the car? You'll need it more than us down there. We got the truck. What's the difference? We don't need two cars."

And so he did. Take the car. On Labour Day weekend, with all his possessions piled into the trunk and the back seat of the family's blue '81 Impala. Stereo, tapes, records, clothes, posters and books. At the gate he paused and tooted the horn twice at his mother and father as they stood in the yard. Then he lurched about ten yards further and stopped and got out and waved. Then he disappeared around the corner.

Mike turned and looked at his wife and said, "I think I'll kill a couple of birds for dinner."

Claire looked at her husband and said, "I've got lamb. We don't need chickens killed."

Mike said, "Yeah. Well. For later. I thought I'd just do in a dozen or two."

And he turned and walked towards the barn and got about ten yards, his wife standing, watching. When he spun around he was smiling. Pointing at her. Said, "Gotcha." Laughing.

His boy half a mile away, cresting the hill by the Esso station, his left elbow resting on the open window, thinking as he drove, that everyone should do this. Everyone should get to drive a car with everything they own piled around them. All alone. Heading towards the horizon. Driving into the future.

DOROTHY

orothy was talking to Dave about business.
"I should have bought a doughnut store when they were cheap," she said.

"You could have bought a doughnut store?" said Dave.

"We all could have bought doughnut stores," said Dorothy. "If we had bought them when they were cheap."

"You wouldn't have been happy running a doughnut store," said Dave.

"Well, I'm not happy running a bookstore," said Dorothy.

It was a Friday night, 9:30. Woodsworth's, Dorothy's bookstore, had been closed since six. For the last two hours Dorothy had been sitting by the cash register in Dave's record store sipping scotch, listening to Gene Ammons and complaining.

"If you had owned a doughnut store you'd be dead," said Dave. "You would have spent the last twelve years eating doughnuts. Your arteries would have plugged up. You would have had a heart attack. And you'd be dead. Or worse."

"Maybe I would have met a cop," said Dorothy.

"Exactly," said Dave.

◧ ◧ ◧

Dorothy said that with what she could get for her house and the store she could probably buy a nice little spot down around Niagara-on-the-Lake. Dave said, yeah, she could open a gift shop and spend her Friday nights wrapping gingham around jam jars. Dorothy said, the way she felt she would be happy to wrap the gingham around herself and work in the fudge store.

It had been building since the fall. A series of little things. The afternoon the man came in and harangued her because she was charging for the Bible. It's God's word, he said. Not yours. There were the sales reps. One of the major houses was sending someone who was driving her nuts. The first time he came she made the mistake of taking him into her office at the back. She couldn't get rid of him. He had pasted the covers of the books he was pitching onto pieces of cardboard and taped notes onto the back of the cardboard. She was trapped for forty-five minutes while he read his sales pitch book by book. The only thing he pitched with any passion was a specialty line called "Greeting Card Books." These were paperbacks with a space on the cover for an address and a stamp. You were supposed to mail the book like a greeting card. Each book came with a pre-printed message on the cover. There were messages for birthdays, graduations, anniversaries, births and deaths. There were three titles to choose from: *The Wizard of Oz, True Experiences in Telepathy* and *Ask Any Girl,* by Winifred Wolfe.

"You're kidding," said Dave.

"I'm just tired of it," said Dorothy. "Tired of the bullshit. Tired of books for Christ's sake."

So tired, thought Dorothy, the next morning, that she had books in her store that she actually hated. A year ago she had, against her better instincts, ordered ten copies of a book called *Teach Your Baby Math: The Revolutionary Discovery that It Is Easier to Teach Math to an Infant than to a Seven-year-old.* A sales rep had convinced her this book was going to be a best-seller. He said they were going to promote it heavily and that it would literally fly off her shelves. It was a year and a half later and there were nine still in the nest. Her nest. It was a fair sign of how bad things were that those nine books were still around. She could have easily returned them, but she kept them right up front—holding on to them the way you might hold on to a sour marriage.

"Who would want to teach a baby math," she hissed one afternoon as she passed the table where the books were piled. She thought she was alone in the store. She hadn't noticed that Tom Brady from the library had stepped in.

"Not me," said Tom breezily from behind a shelf.

That night Dorothy decided if things didn't get better she should get out while she still could.

Dave said, "Think about it."

He didn't want Dorothy to close her bookstore. And not just because he couldn't imagine the block without her. If anyone was made for the book business it was Dorothy Capper. No one loved books like Dorothy. It showed in her store. Ever since she opened it Woodsworth's has been a beacon for booklovers—a lighthouse of literature—a platonic example of the perfect bookstore. People who had never even thought of buying a book had found themselves drawn into the store and been astounded to find themselves leaving with a book tucked under their arm. Many of them returned. And some of them went on to buy things like book shelves and bookmarks and other book accoutrements. Dorothy's store has all the attributes of a good barber shop, or one of those cafés where you stop for coffee in a summer town. You could walk through the door in a bad mood, but it was impossible to stay cranky once you were inside. Woodsworth's had become a home away from home for many people. The perfect place to kill half an hour—at lunch, or on your way home for supper.

Dorothy promised herself a decision about her future by April 1. On the last Friday in March she realized she had four days left. On Saturday morning she went to work looking for a sign. She got three.

The first in the form of seventy-four-year-old Gil Hartley, a retired Presbyterian dairy farmer. He came into the store at eleven o'clock. Dorothy had never seen him before.

"From Drumbolt, Ontario," he said. "Here visiting my grandkids. My wife died last year. Cancer."

"I'm sorry," said Dorothy.

"Me too," said Gil.

He was wearing jeans rolled up at the cuffs, black shoes, a dark green work shirt and a plaid wool jacket. His hands were large and rough. He had big ears.

"I'd like something for my granddaughter's eleventh birthday," he said. Adding quickly, "Tomorrow."

Dorothy nodded.

Gil said, "I left my glasses at home. Maybe you could choose something. Something nice. A book like."

You learn a lot of things in a bookstore over twelve years. One of them is how to sell a book with grace to someone who cannot read. Dorothy went to the back of the store and took down a paperback copy of *Anne of Green Gables*.

"Six dollars and ninety-five cents," she said to Gil Hartley. "I know she will like it."

Gil held the book self-consciously—the way he might hold a baby.

"I read it when I was twelve," said Dorothy. "I liked it a lot. She'll like it. I'm sure."

Gil's wallet was attached to his pants with a long silver chain. He counted out the money. A five, a two and a handful of change. Seventy-four years old—buying his first book.

"I know she'll like it," Dorothy said for the second

time, putting the book in a bag. What else, she wondered, could you buy for seven dollars that could change someone's life? It was the first sale of the day. When Gil left she paid some bills and felt good doing it.

After lunch a woman came in carrying a potted plant. A cyclamen. She wanted to thank Dorothy for referring her to Dr. Cooper at the university. Lesley Cooper ran a women's therapy group. Dorothy had given this woman one of Lesley Cooper's pamphlets when she had bought a book called *The Courage to Heal*.

"She changed my life," said the woman. "I just wanted to say thanks."

Dorothy used to feel uncomfortable selling self-help books. She would bag them the way she imagined druggists must have bagged condoms when she was a child—with dignity but with no acknowledgement of what was being sold. But she had lost her instinctive distrust of the genre. People did learn things from books.

She watched the woman leave the store and looked at the plant, and smiled ruefully.

The catalogue was what pushed her over the edge. It arrived in the mail from California. It was from a company she had never heard of. It was a weird catalogue and she was about to throw it out when she noticed the "How To" section at the end. Three books in particular caught her eye.

How To Beat Honesty Tests
How To Disguise Yourself
How To Create False IDs

She ordered those three. No matter what happened over the next twelve months, waiting to see who would buy them would make getting up in the morning interesting. She would put them in the front where no one could miss them. She looked around at the room full of books. The posters. The table displays. The counter full of gadgets. It was cluttered, but it was her clutter. Her place. She went to the back of the store and picked out another copy of *Anne of Green Gables*. She carried it back to the cash and sat down again and began to read.

A Ton of Fun

With all his experience working in summer camps James Bodak figured he would make a good Big Brother. He thought it would be like being an uncle. He thought working with kids again would be fun.

James was twenty-eight years old. He had been living in Toronto for three years. He moved there from Winnipeg. He was the assistant manager in a downtown branch of the Candian Imperial Bank of Commerce.

James left a girlfriend behind in Manitoba, a grade two teacher named Joanne whom he could not quite marry. Their relationship didn't survive the move. They visited back and forth during James's first year in Toronto. But those weekends, which they both looked forward to with such confidence, more often than not, turned sour before they were over. There were sold-out movies and line-ups at restaurants, a lost wallet and a growing silence that neither of them was used to. One Sunday night James felt a sense of freedom when he dropped Joanne at the airport. The feeling surprised him.

That October Joanne called to say that she wouldn't be coming for Thanksgiving. She didn't offer an explanation, and James didn't ask for one. He had tickets for two plays at Stratford. He took a friend from work instead. James suspected Joanne had met someone else. He was right.

One night not long after, it occurred to James that he might not have children of his own. The thought worried him. But it didn't surprise him. All in all he was content. He was busy at work. He liked his job. He was making new friends. But he missed having kids in his life.

He knew hundreds of kids in Winnipeg from the camp on Lake of the Woods. Even though he had been away from Manitoba for three years he couldn't walk through the Portage Place Mall without a kid recognizing him. Often he didn't remember their names—but he enjoyed being stopped. It made him feel as if he belonged somewhere. He had come to accept that the only kids who were going to stop him in Toronto were going to ask him for spare change.

Big Brothers asked James to come to their offices on a Friday afternoon to meet the boy they had chosen for him. The moment they were introduced, James didn't like the kid. It was a possibility that had not occurred to him.

He was horrified when Jed was ushered into the small meeting room. He couldn't put his finger on it but the moment he saw the boy James wanted to get up and leave. But he couldn't do that.

James tried hard to be a good big brother. He took Jed to a Maple Leaf hockey game, they went bowling and to the zoo. After the initial excitement, however, James began to find the visits more of a chore than he had expected. Eventually the two of them settled on a Friday night routine that they both enjoyed. Jed would come to James's apartment. They would order pizza and watch a video together. It was all right, but it wasn't what James had imagined when he had volunteered. He had wanted someone to love. He had imagined his little brother would look up to him. In fact they had little in common. In fact James found Jed irritating.

One Friday night when he drove Jed home James asked if he could meet his mother. They lived in a basement apartment on College Street. James followed Jed into the dark living room. There was a man and a woman slouched on a couch watching a large television. The volume was too loud to talk over. No one made a move to lower it.

"This is James," said Jed. He was shouting.

Jed's mother, Marilyn, leered up at James. Marilyn was drunk.

"Shut the friggin' TV down," she yelled at the man lying beside her. "Don't you have any friggin' manners?"

The first thing she said to James was: "I'm going to friggin' kick him out of here if he doesn't smarten up." She was talking about the man she was lying beside.

The man said, "Screw off, Marilyn." He was wearing an undershirt and black jeans.

James felt silly standing in the living room talking to Marilyn. He asked Jed to show him his bedroom. Jed and his brother slept in bunk beds in a room at the end of the hall.

"That's my bed," said Jed pointing at the bottom bunk. There was a woman passed out in it.

"Who's that?" asked James.

"That's my aunt," said Jed.

The woman didn't stir.

"I'll sleep on the top bunk tonight, with Wayne," said Jed.

Wayne was Jed's younger brother.

There was one other bedroom. It was uninhabitable. Full of junk: tires, garbage, broken furniture.

"My mother sleeps on the couch with Elwood," said Jed. "She's going to kick him out next week."

James was appalled by the apartment.

On his way home he decided to clean out the second bedroom for Jed.

He arrived on a Friday night with garbage bags and a can of light-blue paint. Jed helped him haul the garbage out of the room and went to watch television. James began painting. Marilyn and Elwood, who hadn't appeared to have moved since the night James had met them, didn't show any interest in what he was doing. They didn't seem to approve or disapprove. They seemed neither surprised nor resentful that he was invading their home. Nothing.

As the night wore on the television got louder and louder. So did the yelling. About ten o'clock there was a scuffle and Marilyn yelled at Elwood to get out.

Elwood didn't leave.

The louder things got, the faster James painted.

He was slopping paint on the walls as if he believed things might settle down as soon as the job was done. It was clear, however, that no one cared whether the room was painted or not. He wondered whether he would have to call the police before the night was over.

This is not what this kid needs, he thought. When he left, the room looked great, but he felt stupid.

That summer James rented a cottage on the Maine coast for two weeks. He asked Marilyn if he could take Jed and Wayne to the ocean.

Marilyn said, "Can Elwood and I come?"

James said, "There's not enough room."

It took three days to drive to Maine. On the way they stopped in upper New York State at the Baseball Hall of Fame. James almost cried in the Hall of Honour when he came across a plaque for Albert Joseph Barlick. Umpire. The plaque said that Barlick had earned the respect of everyone—players included—for his fairness, his knowledge of the rules and his ability to handle rough situations. James hadn't expected to find an official in the hall. Travelling with two young boys was presenting him with his share of rough situations. He wondered what the boys would have to say about *his* fairness. About *his* knowledge of the rules. Mostly he felt over his head.

James and the boys tried a machine that measured how fast you could throw a baseball. You got three tries for a dollar. When he had thrown his three balls, the man running the machine handed James a certificate that looked disturbingly like his degree from the University of Manitoba. It occurred to him that he could frame the certificate and hang it in his office. Fifty-three miles an hour, it read. It was faster than either Wayne or Jed. James quietly folded the paper and slipped it into his pocket after he watched a nine-year-old-girl wearing a Yankees hat drill the ball into the canvas at seventy-one miles an hour.

The cottage only had one bedroom, but it was perfect. The boys slept on two couches in the living room. James had the lumpy double bed to himself. He made rules: no soft drinks, no television, a one-hour nap after lunch. The boys complained but they did what he told them. James watched them swim for hours.

"Look at me," they cried over and over again from the surf. "Look at me."

He made them wear polo pyjamas on the beach so they wouldn't get sunburned. They built sand castles. They went fishing for crabs.

James tried to get them to bed early. To cook them good food. At night he read to them from *A Catcher In The Rye*. They had never heard anything like it.

When their two weeks were up, they drove north into Quebec so they could spend a night in Montreal on their way home. It was falling dark as they drove through the White Mountains. The boys pressed against the back window of the car singing,

One hundred bottles of beer on the wall,
One hundred bottles of beer.

James's muffler was loose. Every time the car went over a bump the muffler bounced on the pavement and sent a shower of sparks into the night and Jed and Wayne squealed with delight. James didn't care a hoot about the muffler. He was happy.

They slept in a motel on the edge of Montreal. The next morning they went to a bank so James could exchange his American currency.

As James was walking out of the bank Jed came running up to him waving an envelope.

"Look what I found," he said. "It was on the floor."

"Let me see that," said James.

Jed held out the envelope.

It was full of money.

"Where did you find this?" asked James, his heart racing, his fingers flipping through the bills.

"By the bank machine," said Jed.

The envelope contained over two thousand dollars.

"We have to take this back," James heard himself saying. "This isn't ours."

The boys looked incredulous.

"It's going back," said James again as if trying to convince himself. He was adding up what the last two weeks had cost him. He was thinking that maybe the envelope of money was God's way of acknowledging what he had done. If I kept it, he thought, it would pay for everything, plus leave a bit for my time.

"We have to take it back," he said. "You two take it back to the bank."

James waited on the sidewalk. He was thinking, if the kids go in there alone they will give them a reward. He wanted them to learn you got rewarded for doing the right thing.

When the kids came out they looked stunned.

"What happened?" James asked.

"We gave it to a lady at the counter. She grabbed it from us and took off."

"What did she say?" he asked. "She must have said something."

"She yelled at us. She said, 'Where did you get that? You shouldn't have that.' Then she grabbed it from us and took off. Why did you make us give it back?"

James didn't know what to say.

They went into a restaurant down the street for breakfast. They sat at the counter. James said, "That was not our money. We had to take it back. The lady shouldn't have spoken to you like that. She was wrong. But we did the right thing. We had to take the money back."

The boys looked at him as if he was speaking a foreign language. In many ways he was. Jed spun around on his stool. He slapped his head.

"You're crazy," he said. "I can't believe you made us take the money back. I can't believe this. You're crazy."

James tried another tack.

"There is a thing called karma," he said slowly. "It

means if you do good things to people, then people will do good things to you. You just did something good. Something good will happen to you. If we had kept that envelope it would have been stealing."

All the time he was talking James was thinking, If they weren't with me and *I'd* found the envelope, would I have taken it back?

"You're crazy," said Jed, "Do you know what we could have done with that money?"

James thought they would tell him candy, sneakers, records.

"We could have bought groceries," said Jed. "I could have bought my mother a rocking chair. We could have bought clothes. We could have paid three months' rent. Our mother is going kill us when we tell her what you made us do."

"No," said James, without conviction. "Your mother is going to be proud of you."

He gave the boys a handful of quarters and sent them to a video parlour. While they played video games he went back to the bank.

He asked to see the manager.

"I have just spent two weeks by the ocean," James began.

The manager looked at him cautiously and fiddled with a pen. There was nothing on his desk. James had the feeling this was not his office. He had the feeling they were in an interview room. He had the feeling the manager had his foot over an alarm.

James kept going.

"I took two little boys to the ocean. From Toronto," he added. "They do not have a lot of money."

The manager shifted uncomfortably.

"Once, in Toronto, I met one of these boys at dinner time. He had not eaten all day. He had not had breakfast and he had not had lunch. He had not eaten because there was no food in his house. For the past two weeks I tried to give them good food and good times. I read to them."

James could hardly speak he was so mad. His voice cracked. Shit, he thought, I am going to cry.

He told the manager about the envelope. He told him what had happened when the boys had returned it.

"What do you want me to do?" asked the manager. He seemed to visibly relax.

"This is what you are going to do," said James.

"I am going to bring the kids back here in a few minutes and you are going to tell them they are heroes.

"You are going to take their names and addresses. You are going to write a letter and thank them for what they have done. You are going to give them each a reward."

"How much of a reward?" asked the manager.

James wasn't ready for this. He didn't know what to say. He wanted to say fifty dollars each. He said twenty dollars.

"Give them twenty dollars," he said.

James was not good with negotiations.

James didn't let the boys open their envelopes until they were on the road.

"Go ahead," he said when they hit the highway.

The boys ripped the envelopes open.

"Ten dollars," said Wayne.

"Ten dollars," said Jed. "Our mother is going to kill us."

It is a six-hour drive from Montreal to Toronto.

"Maybe we did do the right thing," said Wayne eventually.

"Ten dollars," was all Jed could say.

They laughed.

James was still thinking of the $2,300 that got away. Jesus, he thought. He still didn't know what he would have done if the boys had not been with him.

The city looked dirtier than it did when they left. Grimier. James followed the boys into their apartment. They look great, he thought. They have grown. They have put on weight. He was proud of himself.

The kids flew through the door.

"Mom," said Jed. Not Hi. Hello. We're back. It was great. But...

"*We found $2,300 dollars in an envelope. He made us give it back.*"

Jed was pointing at James. James was standing in the living-room like a shoplifter.

"He made you what?" Marilyn was looking at him. "Are you crazy?" she said. "Do you know what I could do with $2,300?"

"See," they said to James together.

See.

The word echoed in James' mind as he drove down Bloor Street. He was looking forward to his apartment. He was looking forward to a night alone and a cold beer. He was wondering if there was any good mail.

Be-Bop-A-Lula

I t was study break. And, as if on cue, spring was in the air. Maybe a record high for this time of year, said the weather man. Maybe, fifteen degrees this afternoon. Dave wore his spring jacket and sneakers to work. Walking out the front door he felt...light. The sun warm on his face for the first time in months.

Morley had taken the kids to Florida.

"It's great," she said on the phone. "I wish you could have come. God, I needed this."

Dave was home alone.

"It's OK," he said. "I'm OK."

But he wasn't OK. Something strange was going on. It began after he drove his family to the airport. It began as a funny whirling feeling in his stomach. It wasn't like he was sick. It was a pleasant sort of feeling. Like being excited. Or nervous. But Dave wasn't feeling excited or nervous about anything. He was feeling... goofy.

At first he thought he was tired. He had stayed up late helping his wife pack. At midnight he had taken the car to the all-night gas station. His family was leaving at seven in the morning. They were at the airport at five-thirty. I must be tired, he thought.

He went to bed early on Wednesday and slept

soundly but when he woke up in the morning the feeling was still there. Except more so.

He felt...giddy.

It was another beautiful day.

"You wouldn't believe the weather," he said to Morley on the phone. "Everyone is outside. It's like someone pulled a switch."

On his way home he bought a bottle of red wine and picked up a video. This is great, he thought. I never get to do this. He cooked pasta and mixed it with garlic and broccoli and drank half the bottle of wine. While he ate he listened to Paganini's Violin Concerto, Number One—occasionaly directing the CD with his fork. After he ate he put on coffee and did the dishes. He was looking forward to watching his movie, but as he was putting the Paganini away he spotted an old Beatles album and the whirling in his stomach intensified. It was the soundtrack from *A Hard Day's Night*. He hadn't listened to the record for years. The summer he was sixteen he had gone to England with his parents and he had brought the album back with him. It was possible that he had been the first person in the country to own it. He pulled the record out of the jacket and spun it between his palms.

That first dissonant chord filled the kitchen like an old friend. Dave wondered whether aficionados were still arguing over whether the chord was an F major or G major 7th. In his book *A Day In The Life* Mark Hertsgaard writes that the swelling opening chord of the album sounds like a hijacked church bell announcing the party of the year. Dave smiled, turned up the volume, sat down at the table and poured himself another glass of wine. After all these years. The music washed over and through him. He played the album twice and then got down on his hands and knees and pawed about and finally found "Abbey Road."

He killed the bottle of wine sitting on the floor listening to the second side of the album. The side with the incomplete song fragments. He had forgotten how much he loved the way the uncompleted songs had been mixed into one glorious fifteen-minute movement. Woven together like that because McCartney and Lennon hadn't had the stomach to work as a team any more and couldn't finish writing the individual numbers.

He staggered to bed after midnight. He never watched his movie.

On Friday, when he woke up, he didn't want to listen to CBC radio. He reached over and sleepily changed the station to CHUM—hits of the fifties and sixties—the music of *his* life. He brushed his teeth to Paul Simon's "Kodachrome." When he was eating breakfast they played the title song from the musical *Hair.* He ran his hand over his head.

He felt...buoyant.

All day at work old pop tunes kept bouncing into his imagination. He didn't know what the hell was going on but he liked the way he was feeling. He usually played jazz in the store. On Friday he played rock and roll all day long.

Rock and roll had once been a big part of Dave's life. But lately his tastes had shifted. He had become more aligned with the likes of Gershwin and Billie Holiday. Louis Armstrong. Gene Ammons. He had even, to his own surprise, brought home a Tony Bennett record earlier in the year.

He had left rock and roll behind him.

As a teenager he had spent hours gazing into Renee Atwater's eyes, strumming a guitar and singing Beatles tunes.

Actually the guitar was imaginary. Actually he was staring into his bedroom mirror, not Renee's eyes—but it was almost as good.

As an adult these private performances had evolved into grander and more theatrical moments. Dave had a favourite Sondheim album which had a live-audience track. He would put it on and then run out of the room and wait for the applause to begin. As it built he would walk into the living-room with his head down and then, as the audience went wild, he would acknowledge the cheers and smile coyly at someone in the upper balcony. A friend perhaps. Maybe Renee Atwater. She is married, and she hasn't seen him for years, and when she does, even from way up in the balcony, she thinks of what might have been and her heart breaks. Dave always dedicates the third number on the album to her. I'd like to sing this one for someone special, he'd say. Someone I used to sing to a long time ago.

When his son Sam was very young Dave would involve him in these shows. He would hold him over his head and present him to the crowd and they would go crazy when they realized he had a child. Eventually Sam got too heavy and he couldn't use him in his shows any more.

Dave kept the radio on CHUM all weekend. At night he sat in the kitchen playing old records. He was working his way back down the evolutionary chain of rock and roll. Not into the authentic blues stuff he knew he should be listening to, but down the glorious tributary where he had paddled as a kid.

Neil Sedaka's "Happy Birthday, Sweet Sixteen," The Happenings' "See You in September," Lesley Gore's "It's My Party and I'll Cry If I Want To," and while he made supper, "Leader of the Pack" by The Shangri-Las. Dave was in pop heaven. It all sounded good to him. His sense of discrimination and good taste were blown away by a primal memory that was almost physical. He was in the elevator of adolescence and it was descending— dropping deeper by the hour. Twenty, nineteen, eighteen, seventeen, sixteen! He was dancing around the kitchen singing,

Dook, Dook, Dook,
Dook of Earl

He was banging his hand on the steering wheel. Christ, he was having a good time.

On Monday and Tuesday the whirling feeling in his stomach was with him all day long. He was moving in a kind of dopey haze. He wasn't paying attention to any details. He was…grooving. Suddenly his life was only coloured in primary colours.

Debbie Anderson, the girl who came in on Wednesday and Friday nights had, since he hired her, been his favourite part-timer. Debbie had short blonde hair, an elfish smile, big brown eyes. She went to the University of Toronto. She wanted to be a phys-ed teacher.

On Wednesday night when they were closing Dave said, "Have you had dinner? I'm going to El Basha for falafel if you want to come. Morley's away," he added.

"I have to study," Debbie said. "I have a physics test tomorrow."

On Thursday Dave woke up at six-thirty without the alarm. He felt bright and alert. It was the second day in a row it had happened. Didn't the Monkees have a song about that? It wasn't even seven and he was…excited. He turned on the radio.

The Loving Spoonful—"A Younger Girl Keeps Coming Across My Mind." He thought about Debbie. He wished she had gone to dinner with him. He imagined the two of them walking down the street together. Wondered what it would be like to hold her. Maybe he would ask her again on Friday.

On Friday morning while he was shaving he was surprised to see a blemish on his cheek. A small red dot had appeared on his face overnight. He didn't pay any attention to it at first but as he was leaving the house he thought about it again and went back to the bathroom to check. A pimple? He hadn't had a pimple in years. He got to the front door again and was about to pull it shut behind him when the thought crashed down on him. He was forty-five years old. Forty-five-year-olds didn't get pimples. They got skin cancer. He was back in the house in a flash. He found Morley's magnifying make-up mirror. Was that how it happened? You woke up one morning and you had skin cancer? What else could it be?

Dave couldn't get the blemish out of his mind. He checked it three times before lunch. He thought about phoning Dr. Freeberg and having her look at it, but what if it *was* a pimple? He didn't want to risk sitting in his doctor's office and hearing her tell him that. He wished Morley was home so he could show it to her.

Like many men, Dave has a complicated relationship with his body. He inhabits it the way a nervous traveller settles into a commercial airliner—carefully monitoring every arrhythmia—continually aware that only through a force of his will does it stay in the air. When Dave and Morley got married Dave's friend Dorothy suggested the minister change the marriage vow for Dave's turn. Change it from…"in sickness and in health," to "in sickness and in remission." Funny, said Dave, very funny.

He couldn't help what his mind did with a list of symptoms.

The cancer, as he had come to think of it, prayed on his mind all day. By closing time he had decided to treat it symptomatically—like a pimple—if it wasn't better by the time Morley got back he'd go to the doctor. He wasn't going to show it to Morley. She wouldn't take it seriously.

He had planned to hang around until closing. He had planned to ask Debbie out for a drink. Instead he asked her about the blemish.

"Do you think this is skin cancer?" he said.

She looked at Dave and then at the spot on his face. Then she laughed and said, "Oh yeah. All the skin cancers I've seen started out like that."

Dave left at six. Alone.

He went to the drugstore and picked up a tube of Clearasil. As he headed towards the cash he looked around to see if he knew anyone in the store. He felt like he was buying a pack of condoms and he wanted to do it privately. He walked around to make sure he was safe.

His heart froze when he saw the blood-pressure chair. It was in the corner at the back of the store. Over the years Dave had had his blood pressure tested on a number of occasions. Dr. Freeberg had always reported a more or less normal reading. Dave suspected that these normal readings were not an accurate reflection of reality. They were always taken after he had been left in the waiting room for twenty, thirty minutes. Why shouldn't he be relaxed? He suspected that the normal readings were, in all likelihood, abnormal. Sometimes, when he was upset, he felt his blood pounding in his ears. Surely that wasn't normal. He decided his blood pressure was variable and dependent on stimuli beyond his control. He had never had an opportunity to check his theory.

That's why the chair terrified him. It was one thing to suspect you had high blood pressure. It was another thing to know it. Dave didn't want his body to know its own blood pressure. He didn't want his body to be given strategic information at the cellular level that it could use against him. He suspected that if his body knew how close it was to making the leap from borderline to hypertense it would abandon everything else—all the various viruses and bacterias—and launch a frontal assault on his circulatory system.

The blood-pressure machine looked like a self-service electric chair. There was a slot on the armrest to slip your arm through and a cuff that presumably inflated when you started the machine.

Dave was aware that if he sat down and surrendered his arm to the machine horrible things could happen. Someone who knew him could waltz in as the machine was printing his score. The idea of Dorothy Capper knowing that his diastolic blood pressure was north of 180 horrified Dave more than the implications of the information. He knew it didn't make sense but he felt if no one, including him, knew what his blood pressure was, then it didn't count. It was like cheating on a diet.

There was a stack of instruction pamphlets beside the machine. Dave slipped one into his pocket. He didn't read it until he was out on the street. It opened up a whole new realm of possibilities…including step-by-step instructions of what he should do if his reading was zero over zero. Something even Dave had not imagined. He forgot about Debbie Anderson. He went out to supper, then, instead of going home, he went back to the drugstore and cruised by the chair the way he had cruised by Renee Atwater's house when he was a teenager. He felt the same way. Oppressed, anxious, hopeful, hopeless.

Just thinking about the chair raised his blood pressure. He knew that he was going to try it. He knew he wouldn't be able to stop himself. For the next three days he kept returning to the drugstore and stood in front of the chair like a poor dumb sick moose standing in the middle of a housing development. He couldn't stop himself. It was like trying to keep his tongue away from a sore in his mouth. He knew he was doomed. He also knew that he would have to try it when there was no possibility of anyone seeing him.

He decided early morning would be best.

The drugstore opened at nine.

Two days later Dave showed up ten minutes before opening time.

He waited on the far side of the street.

He felt like a bank robber.

When they unlocked the doors he was the first person in the store. It couldn't take more than a minute to do the test, he thought. He could be in and gone before anyone saw him. He went right to the chair. He rolled up his sleeve. He sat down. He put his arm through the metal slot. He pushed the large green button that said BEGIN TEST. He felt the rubber cuff inflate and tighten around his forearm.

He felt his heart pounding.

And then he felt an excrutiating pain run down his arm.

Christ. He was having a heart attack.

The machine was squeezing him tighter than he thought it should. Surely it shouldn't feel like this. Surely it shouldn't hurt.

He tried to pull his arm out of the cuff.

It wouldn't come.

He pulled again.

Still it wouldn't budge.

He looked at the black screen. It was like the screen on a bank machine. It began flashing his score in bright red numbers. 130/75. Not bad. Better than he thought. Well within normal limits.

OK, thought Dave. Now, let me go. But it didn't. It wouldn't.

Dave felt panic surge through him. He was trapped in the chair. He pulled again, more recklessly this time. Still nothing. He looked at the screen. His blood pressure had risen to 135/78.

Shit.

He tried to relax.

Then he jerked his arm violently.

Still nothing.

Now his blood pressure was 140/80. That was borderline hypertense.

Oh God, he thought. This is crazy. He tried to calm himself again. He sat for a full minute without moving. He tried to figure out what was wrong. Something had happened to the machine. The rubber cuff would not deflate. And until it deflated the metal slot which was holding his arm to the chair would not release him. Maybe there is some button I am supposed to push, he thought. Maybe there is a release button somewhere. He couldn't see a release button.

He pulled his arm again. Still nothing. He didn't know what to do. Collect your thoughts, Dave. What is the worst thing that could happen? Someone could see him. Someone he knew could see him.

No.

The store could catch fire. He wondered if he could stand up and hump his way out of the store with the chair attached to him. He imagined getting as far as the check-out counter and then getting wedged in the aisle by the cash register. He thought of dying of smoke inhalation by the cash register, with a blood-pressure chair attached to his back like a tortoise's shell. It was the kind of trivial death that Dave had always feared. Like being hit by a diaper truck. The kind of death where his friends would gather quietly in some solemn funeral parlour until someone started to giggle. He didn't want people giggling at his funeral. He wanted a death with dignity.

He began to struggle so violently that the chair started rocking.

He heard a man's voice say, "What's going on over there?"

Dave looked at the screen. The red numbers were blinking like the clock on a broken VCR. Except they were ascending. His blood pressure had sailed through borderline and was now firmly entrenched in hypertense. 160/93.

Dave looked up and saw Bill Turner, the pharmacist, heading towards him.

To his horror, behind Bill, he saw Debbie Anderson.

He felt his heart accelerate.

He glanced at the screen.

172/90.

This was a nightmare. He had the blood pressure of a seventy-five-year-old man.

He twisted desperately in the chair and reached for the screen with his left hand—trying to cover the blinking red numbers the way a man caught outside his house with no clothes on might cover his groin. He felt naked, exposed, humiliated. Debbie and Bill Turner arrived at the chair at the same time.

"Hi," said Dave, smiling weakly, still trying to cover the screen.

"I'm stuck," said Dave. "I can't get my arm out."

Bill was staring at Dave as if he had asked him for spare change.

"See," he said, rattling his arm. "It won't come out."

He could feel the blood pounding in his ears.

He felt like he was going to faint.

I am not going to faint, he said to himself.

"Hi, Dave," said Debbie cheerily.

Then she said, "Your nose is bleeding."

Dave's left hand involuntarily flew away from the screen. He brought it up to his face and when he took it away he saw blood on his fingers.

And then everyone turned simultaneously from his red hand to the red numbers blinking on the now uncovered screen. The numbers reminded Dave of the digital displays they have in modern elevators. Sadly, the elevator was going up. The three of them watched the screen blink from 172 up to, and through, 180. It settled at 181.

"Geez, Dave," said Bill Turner. "Are you OK?"

"I can't get my arm out," said Dave for the third time.

Dave felt a drop of blood land in his lap.

"I'll get you some Kleenex," said Debbie.

The fire department arrived forty-five minutes later. By then Dave's blood pressure had settled at 178/95.

"Geez," said the fire chief, looking at the screen. "Are you OK?"

The drugstore had taken on the festive feel of an accident scene. There were about fifteen people standing in a circle around the chair. Every few minutes someone new arrived and there was a blush of whispering as they asked what was going on.

After twenty more minutes of fiddling with the

chair the chief sent a man out to the truck to get the Jaws of Life. They were going to cut Dave out.

"Wait a minute," said Bill Turner. "You're going to wreck the chair."

"For Christ's sake Bill," said Dave. "I'll pay for it. Just get me out of here."

It took five minutes. Everyone applauded when Dave stood up. He rubbed his arm carefully and said he was fine and looked at his watch and said he had to go. People slapped him on the back as he pushed through the crowd—as if he had just won a race or something.

Debbie Anderson said, "I'll see you Wednesday."

His family came back two nights later. He drove out to the airport to pick them up. He left the headlights on in the parking garage and by the time they had corralled their suitcases and gone to the washroom and everyone got out to the car the battery had gone dead. It took Dave half an hour to find someone to give them a boost.

After they got the kids to bed, Dave said to Morley, "I have something to tell you. Something you better hear from me."

He never took Debbie Anderson out to dinner. He still liked her but he felt old whenever she was around. The red blemish on his face disappeared a week after Morley got home. He never mentioned it.

POLAROIDS

obin spent the Christmas before he died where he spent all his Christmases—at his family's cottage in Muskoka. He flew to Toronto, from Vancouver, arriving in the early evening on the afternoon of December 21st. He called his parents the week before and said don't come to meet me at the airport. I'll rent a car. Bob and Sandra were already up north. They said, are you sure? Robin said, yes, I'm sure. But he regretted it when he arrived at the airport. He seemed to be the only one waiting for luggage who didn't have someone to hug him, drive him home.

He was going to spend the next two nights alone at his parents' house in town. He picked up his rental car and on his way home stopped and bought fresh-cut flowers from a Korean grocer—his favourites, gladioli. He always kept fresh-cut flowers in his apartment in Vancouver. When he got to the house he divided the flowers between two vases. He set one on his mother's bureau—so the flowers were the first thing he would see when he woke up. He had decided to sleep in his parents' room instead of his own. It was a gesture of extravagance. The second vase he set in his mother's sewing room.

He laid his clothes out on his father's bed. His socks

lined up by colour, his shirts fanned like a hand of cards. It looked like a display in a fancy clothing store—the effect pleased him. He did some Christmas shopping, had dinner with old friends and sat in the sewing room sipping vodka martinis and looking at the family photo albums.

The night before he left for the cottage he peeled back the cellophane from one page and removed a photo. He put it in his Day-Timer. It was a Polaroid of him and Christopher sitting on a couch at his parents' cottage. His mother had taken the picture two Christmases ago. In the picture Robin is wearing a bold striped soccer jersey, jeans and loafers with no socks. He is smiling. He has a moustache. His hair is cut short. He looks neat. He was thirty-two years old. Christopher was twenty-eight.

⊠ ⊠ ⊠

On Christmas eve Robin picked Cathy up in front of the Plaza Two—a high-rise hotel on Bloor Street built on top of The Bay. Cathy was standing by the Salvation Army man, wearing a green suede coat with fur trim at the collar and the wrists. There was a black leather suitcase on the sidewalk beside her and a green nylon bag over her shoulder. When she spotted Robin's rented blue Cavalier, Cathy flicked her cigarette onto the sidewalk. She stepped on it on her way to the car.

This will be the first time Robin has brought a girl

home for Christmas. Bob and Sandra, who have never met Cathy, aren't sure what to make of the visit.

"I'm not sure what she does," said Sandra, to her neighbour, Elise, at bridge the week before. "We haven't heard too much about her. He phoned last month and asked if he could bring someone for Christmas. We thought he meant his friend Christopher. He came two years ago. And then he told us it was a girl."

"Must be serious," said Elise. "If they bring them home for Christmas it's usually serious."

It was falling dark when Robin turned onto Howland Avenue. The coloured lights glowing on the balconies of the large Annex houses remind him of when his mother and father used to drive around looking at Christmas decorations. He wondered if families did that any more. He flicked the heater on and smiled at Cathy.

"You can work the radio," he said.

When they get to MacTier, Robin drives off the highway and parks in front of the IGA. His mother has asked him to pick up some hamburger meat. A lot of families with nearby cottages buy frozen beef from Gerry Jones and take it back to the city—which of course is where Gerry buys most of his meat in the first place. If the steaks are no different than what they could get in town, the service is. Gerry enjoys talking about his trade. Later that night as she unwraps the hamburger Sandra will tell Cathy that some butchers add liver to ground beef to make it look better.

"The blood from the liver makes the meat redder," she will say.

Cathy will say that liver makes her throw up. You know?

Robin wanders around the narrow aisles and buys four packages of smoked oysters, some blue cheese and the latest edition of the *Parry Sound Beacon*. Cathy wrinkles her nose at the cheese and buys a pack of gum. A young boy in a blue apron offers to carry their bag to the car.

Sitting in the parking lot, the headlights on, the engine idling, Robin reaches into his pocket and pulls out a small box. It is gift wrapped.

It is an engagement ring. Bought a week before at Eaton's in Vancouver.

Cathy has to struggle to get the ring over her knuckle but it fits. She has never had a ring on that finger before.

"Wow," she says, holding her hand up in front of her face. "We're engaged. Nice ring."

She is thinking, He didn't have to gift wrap it. That was nice.

Then she looked at Robin and said, "Do we sleep together, or what?"

"There's a guest room," says Robin. "You'll be in the guest room."

⊠ ⊠ ⊠

Cathy's first trick, she didn't know she was doing it for money. It was the afternoon she had sex with Frank who managed the McDonald's where she was working. They went upstairs so they could look at next month's schedule and they ended up doing it on the floor in front of Frank's desk. When it was over Frank took out his wallet, which he kept closed with two elastic bands, and gave her forty bucks. Christ. She thought they were doing it because he liked her. But she didn't say anything and she pocketed the forty. She was sort of scared of Frank.

She went to the drugstore on the way home and spent the money—bought expensive bubble bath from Sweden.

Counting Frank she had slept with four guys by the time she was sixteen. Five if you included her father.

First time she was twelve. The guy, she couldn't remember his name, was seventeen. She met him at the lake where her parents rented a cottage every summer. They used to go up for two or three weeks, and on weekends. She met the guy there and they started going out. She thought she loved him.

One day, in grade ten, when she was sixteen, her friend Ronnie called and said, "I have something to tell you but you can't tell anyone."

Ronnie and Cathy used to be best friends but they weren't best friends anymore. Ronnie was hanging around with the wrong crowd. Cathy knew what she was going to tell her. No, that's not true. She didn't know, but when Ronnie told her Cathy wasn't surprised.

Ronnie had hinted at it on the phone but wouldn't say it right out. She said if you tell anyone people are going to come and get you.

Ronnie lived across the street. She had a big house. Ronnie's mother was a secretary and her father was the manager of a supermarket. Ronnie and Cathy sat on her bed. It had a white comforter. There was a little gold seat in the corner of the room where she kept her Teddy bear collection.

They closed the door and Ronnie put on a George Michael tape. Finally she said,

"I've been hanging around with these guys and they are really good to me. They give me whatever I want. All I have to do is work."

Cathy said, "It's not worth it."

Ronnie said, "It's not as bad as people say. You can make so much money and you meet new people. You don't feel what they're doing or anything."

Cathy said, "I don't care. It's gross."

That Friday they both told their parents they were going to a movie. They went to a Chinese restaurant on Dundas Street instead. They ordered spring rolls and drank two beers each and then Ronnie said, "I'm going to go and work. Why don't you come and watch?"

Cathy already knew that this was what they were

going to do. She sat on the steps of a church watching the cars drive by and Ronnie standing on the corner. Ronnie didn't look scared.

And then a guy stopped and said, "Who's that?"

And Ronnie looked over at Cathy and said, "That's my friend."

And the guy said, "She looks interesting."

Ronnie walked over and said, "Do you want to go with him?"

Cathy was so scared she was shaking.

And Ronnie said, "It's not hard. You should go."

Cathy got in the car and they drove around for a while. When the man asked what her name was she said, "Tracy."

He said, "That's a nice name."

They parked behind a theatre and he gave her sixty dollars and sat back. She started to open his fly like Ronnie told her but she didn't have to do anything else because he finished before she even touched him. She said, "Too bad."

He was mad but she got to keep the money. She thought, this is easy. I could do this all the time. I could make so much money.

That night at home she made a mark on the calendar in her bedroom. A big star. Later she coloured the whole day in—made it a big black square—a day to remember.

That was the only night she stood on a corner. The next Friday a guy in a car picked her up and asked if she wanted to make real money.

"A hundred dollars each time. More."

He had an office and three apartments in the Plaza Two. Two afternoons a week she had to go to the office and answer the phones. There were eight other girls. They were all older than her. One of them was over twenty. She met customers in the apartments. After they were finished, the men left the money on the bureau. She had to stay behind and change the bed. Once a week she had to vacuum. She told her parents she was babysitting. She moved out when she was seventeen. She quit school after grade eleven. By then her parents had split up and they didn't care any more. She got her own apartment. Sometimes she would travel. Go to places like Montreal or Buffalo. When she was twenty-two she started taking courses in the mornings. She wanted to keep her mind going. She figured if she looked after herself and didn't take drugs she could keep working until she was thirty, thirty-five. She saved her money. When she was twenty-three she bought a condominium and opened an account with one of her clients who was a stockbroker. She wasn't going to be broke and have to work a real job. Sometimes she did seven, eight tricks a night.

Her father got remarried to a woman she hated and her mother moved to Hamilton and wouldn't talk to her any more.

The tip of her cigarette glows in the dark car. The smoke curls up around her face. She puts her feet on the dashboard.

"I quit once," she says as she exhales through her lips—blowing the air out so she makes a noise.

"I didn't smoke for two and a half years. Ronnie, she was my roommate?" Cathy stated the fact as a question. As if she needed assurance that she was getting her story right.

"Uh huh," says Robin.

"Ronnie was quitting so I quit with her."

"How?"

"What?"

"How'd you quit?"

"Just stopped." She takes another long drag from her cigarette and looks at it as she exhales. "I guess you gotta have a better reason if it's going to work."

"What was Ronnie's reason?"

"Ronnie? She quit because she didn't want wrinkles. She had little lines by her eyes that used to drive her crazy. She quit because of the lines."

"Huh."

"Ronnie wasn't afraid of dying. Ronnie was afraid of growing old. She said they should change the warnings on the packages. Like, 'SMOKING WILL WRINKLE YOUR FACE.' She said that would stop people."

"What's she doing now."

"Who?"

"Ronnie."

"I don't know."

"She smoking?"

"I don't know."

Cathy was beginning to relax. She was starting to enjoy this. This is cinchy, she thought. She held the ring up so she could see it in the dashboard light.

"You ever do it with a girl?" she asked.

⊠ ⊠ ⊠

Robin went to Upper Canada College for the last three years of high school. He was not good at team sports. He looked awkward, not graceful, when he tried to hit a ball with a baseball or cricket bat. He wasn't a good skater. He couldn't throw a football. Bob thought he should send his son to a school that would toughen him up.

There was nothing at the school he was good at. He managed a minor role in the school play, and felt embarrassed the night his mother came to see him— standing in the background, with only one line to draw attention to himself. He dropped off the Quintilian Club—the school's debating society—after an inter-school debate on prostitution: "Resolve prostitution should be legal." Robin argued for the affirmative and during his speech and his rambling rebuttal he referred to "brothels" as "brummels"—over and over again.

No one said anything and Robin didn't realize his error until he showed his speech to his mother and she said, "What's a brummel?"

He didn't go to the next debate. He said his parents were going up north, which was true, but he could have stayed in town. For years he would feel ashamed whenever he thought of that night. He could see himself, full of adolescent earnestness, waving his hands and ranting on about "brummels."

It was Christopher, years later, who pointed out that the reason no one had corrected him—not his partner, not the opposition, and not even the teacher, Mr. Powell—was not because they wanted to spare him embarrassment—but because no one was game to admit they didn't know what a "brummel" was. They assumed Robin knew something about prostitution they didn't know. Christopher said the whole incident—including Robin quitting the team—was a lesson in human insecurity, especially where matters of sexuality were concerned.

Robin went to Muskoka every weekend—so he wasn't available for the drinking parties where he might have made friends. He learned to drink from his mother—mixing martinis for her and carrying them into the living-room on a black lacquered tray. By the time he was fourteen he had begun to mix extra and leave it in a juice glass in the kitchen for himself. He liked the fuzzy light-headed feeling it gave him.

Mostly what he learned at school was how to be alone, which wasn't such a bad lesson, but it wasn't what Bob was paying three thousand dollars a year to achieve.

Robin only went to one UCC dance. It was the Christmas he was in grade twelve.

Bobby Howard wanted Robin to take his sister Brenda. Brenda went to Branksome Hall and Bobby had promised her he would get her to the dance.

Robin didn't want to admit to Bobby, or anyone else, that he couldn't get his own date. He worried about arriving with Brenda, who he assumed was a loser, otherwise why would Bobby be fixing her up with someone like him? He didn't want to go to the dance as one-half of a loser couple, so he said, I already have a date. He said he was bringing a girl from the lake. He wanted to phone Susan Bailey, a flat-chested girl who had appeared that summer with red hair, a blue bathing suit and a happy smile. Robin thought she was beautiful and thought his reputation could only improve with Susan Bailey by his side. But he was afraid to phone her. One afternoon he stood across the street from her house for two and a half hours. He was hoping he would bump into her: "Susan. Hey. There's a dance at my school this Friday. Do you want to go?"

As if it didn't matter if she went or not.

But he never saw her.

So he practised what he should say on the telephone.

When he finally called, impelled by the looming deadline more than by courage (it was three days until the dance), he hung up when he heard her voice.

So when Friday night came he didn't have a date.

He left home wearing grey flannel pants, a Harris

tweed sports jacket and a blue and white striped shirt
with a tab collar. His father drove him to school and
Robin waited outside watching the tail-lights until they
were out of sight. Then, instead of going into the
school, he walked down Avenue Road to Bloor Street
where he got on the subway, westbound, and rode to
the Spadina Station. There was a community dance at
the United Church near Spadina and Bloor. It cost five
dollars to get in. There was only one girl in the hall
who wasn't wearing jeans. She was a gangly girl in a
green taffeta dress. He waited for a slow song so they
could talk while they were dancing.

"There's a dance at UCC," he said. "Do you want to
go?"

He didn't even know her name.

"Haven't you got a date?" she asked.

"Yeah," said Robin. "But she's sick."

Her name was Pam. He told her if anyone asked she
should say she knew him from the lake.

"Why did you choose me?" she asked, in the taxi on
the way back to UCC.

"Because you were the only one wearing a dress," he
said.

He was twenty before he got kissed. That was the summer his father got him a construction job in
Peterborough. Robin found a basement apartment in a
small clapboard house on Park Street. Every morning
when he got up, every night before he went to bed, he
had to duck his head to miss a heating vent as he

wheeled between the furnace and the washer on his way to the bathroom.

Vic and Evelyn lived upstairs with their seventeen-year-old son Darryl. One Saturday afternoon Darryl, who made pocket money roto-tilling people's gardens with his parent's roto-tiller, asked Robin to join him and his girlfriend on a double date.

It was 1979. Darryl owned a second-hand Chevrolet Impala that was as big as a cruise ship. The shiplike effect was intensified by the purple running lights that Darryl had installed on the dashboard.

Darryl wanted to go to the Demolition Derby.

Robin suggested the movies.

John Wayne is playing, he said. *The Alamo.* It's at The Mustang.

Nancy, his date, looked horrified.

"The Mustang," she said, "is a drive-in."

"So?" said Robin.

That made it better didn't it?

Robin had only been to a drive-in once in his life—with his parents in New England. He was five years old. He fell asleep in the back of the car.

"I promised my boyfriend I wouldn't go to The Mustang. With anyone," said Nancy.

"Haven't you broken up with him?" said Robin.

"Yes. But just since last weekend."

Robin didn't understand the rules. Didn't understand that in Peterborough asking a girl to The Mustang was like asking her to sleep with you. Robin wanted to see John Wayne in *The Alamo*. His father went on and on about Davy Crockett. Davy Crockett was bigger than the Beatles, he said. Took his mother on a vacation once to Texas to visit the Alamo—a disappointment. It was right in the middle of town—like a church or something. Right around the corner from a McDonald's. Can you believe it? Bob had a complete set of Davy Crockett trading cards which he kept on a shelf in his study. Had been furious when Robin was ten years old and he found him playing with them.

"Those things are worth enough to put you through college," he thundered sweeping the cards off the table.

No one except Darryl wanted to go to the Demolition Derby.

No one except Robin had a better idea.

The Mustang was on the edge of Peterborough, where Highway 28 intersects with Highway 7.

This is great, thought Robin as the four of them stepped out into the summer evening. The sky was grey, dipping to black.

Robin and Darryl said they would go to the snack bar. As they wound across the field, through the lines of parked cars, Robin could hear crows calling the night down on them, sense them flapping off into the thickening darkness. The snack bar had a screen window that was raised and lowered every time food or money changed hands. There was a wooden counter and a yellow strip of fly paper hanging beside a single yellow light bulb. The counter was speckled with salt and pools of vinegar. Robin got a milkshake for himself—vanilla—and an order of French fries with gravy for Nancy. On his way back to the car Robin ate three French fries. The rhythmic chirping of cicadas in the surrounding fields was overlaid by thin strands of rock and roll from a hundred car radios. This is great, thought Robin, great. A great place to see a movie. The best place.

They flipped for the front seat. Robin and Nancy won. Robin sat on the passenger side. Nancy sat behind the wheel. She was a large girl. Larger than Robin by twenty, maybe thirty pounds. She was wearing a loose-fitting sweatshirt that hung over her jeans.

And now, now that the movie was almost half over, she was confused. When she resigned herself to the drive-in, Nancy resigned herself to the moves she was sure were coming. By the time they got to The Mustang she had decided what she was going to do. She would let Robin put his arm around her if he wanted, but she wasn't going to kiss him. Not a French kiss anyway. If he tried to stuff his tongue into her mouth Nancy was going to bite it.

The movie was stupid. As it wound tediously along she kept glancing at Robin. He was slouched against the door—leaning away from her—his feet on the dashboard, his eyes glued to the screen. From the back of the car she could hear the fumbling rustle of clothing. Darryl and Peggy were lying across the seat—a tangle of legs and arms—the stupid movie long forgotten.

She felt a tickle of...what was that?

Jealousy?

Jealousy?

What was the matter with her anyway?

She revised her plans. Nothing drastic.

They could kiss if he wanted. Nothing wrong with that. She would let him kiss her—but nothing more.

She stole another peek at him. He was cute. Tall. Skinny. What the hell was the matter? Why wasn't he trying anything?

On the screen in front of her the siege of the Alamo, to which she had been paying less and less attention, was intensifying. Five blue-jacketed Mexican soldiers were loading a cannon. One of the men humped a large round cannon-ball over to the lip of the gun and tipped the ball down the shaft. The captain, or the man in charge, whatever he was, leaned over the cannon and touched the fuse with the punk. The camera zoomed in on the sputtering wick for a moment then panned along the long hard cannon and stopped on the mouth a second before it exploded.

Nancy couldn't stand it any longer. As the cannon-ball flew towards the Alamo she launched herself across the front seat and threw her arms around Robin. She came at him so fast that the handle for the window dug painfully into his back. She began to kiss him. He could smell gravy on her breath. He was horrified. THIS was his first kiss?

She was fumbling with his hair. He felt like he was being smothered. He didn't like this. He didn't want to make out with this girl. He wanted to see the end of

STORIES FROM THE VINYL CAFE

the movie. He wanted to see Davy Crockett killed.

Nancy began to moan. Robin removed her hand from his ear.

"What's the matter," she asked.

"I…I want to see the movie," he said. "I want to watch the movie." He said it twice.

"What's the matter with me?" asked Nancy.

"Nothing," said Robin. But he said it too fast. "Nothing's the matter with you. I just want to watch the movie."

It wasn't to be. Nancy said she had to be home before midnight. Before Santa Anna's troops swarmed over the walls of the monastery. Before the famous last scene. It was one of the worst nights of Robin's life. He still hasn't seen Davy Crockett die.

Robin fell in love during his last year at university. He wasn't surprised that the object of his passion was a twenty-seven-year-old teaching assistant—a graduate student who ran a seminar in romantic poets. Nor was he surprised that he was a man. Bob Jones walked into the conference room and Robin felt his heart accelerate. They lived together for a year and a half. Until Robin caught Bob necking with a freshman at a party. He had been alone for four years—then he met Christopher in Vancouver. There had been no one special since Christopher died in his arms a year ago.

⊞ ⊞ ⊞

Cathy says, "You got any brothers or sisters?"

She is remembering when she was a little girl, eight, maybe nine, driving in the car with her parents. Her mother is screaming at her father.

Her father says, "Look how fat you are. Look at your fat ass spread out on the seat. You couldn't find another man unless you lost thirty, maybe forty pounds."

She used to lie in bed at night and dream that her parents would get a divorce so her father could marry someone else and she could have a little sister.

◼ ◼ ◼

Sandra grabbed her son and kissed him on the lips as he walked into the steaming cottage kitchen.

Cathy hung back by the door startled by the exuberant affection. Overwhelmed by this woman who thought it was appropriate to wear gold earrings and a brooch in her country home.

The cottage was as lavish as Sandra's make-up. There was a fire in the fireplace and a tree by the corner window that looked out at the lake. There were Christmas cards strung around the living-room and a flock of candle choir boys that appeared to be marching across the mantelpiece. They have had these candles since Robin was a boy. Never lit. Twenty-five, thirty Christmases.

"You can put one on my coffin," says Sandra, laughing, after a dinner of home-made tourtière, salad and red wine, "and light it as they lower me into the ground."

After supper Bob does the dishes—he won't let anyone help—and then they play hearts by the fireplace and talk about the theatre—plays Robin has been to in Vancouver—shows Bob and Sandra have seen in New York City.

"I like late-night television," says Cathy, defiantly. "The ones that look like talk shows but are really ads. My favourite is the one for the juicer."

Sandra can't tell by her tone whether the girl is being serious or ironic. Bob, who himself sits up late at night in front of the television, nods.

Cathy says, "I used to like the religious shows. But I'm sort of afraid of them now."

"You're afraid of them?" says Sandra.

"I'm afraid if I start watching one I won't be able to turn it off? I used to love Jimmy Bakker best of all. I sure do miss Jimmy Bakker."

"He got out of jail last month," says Bob. "He's going to start preaching again. With his daughter. They're all crooks."

"What about Tammy Faye?" says Cathy. "What ever happened to Tammy Faye?"

"Married again," says Bob.

"Jimmy Swaggart is pretty good," says Cathy. "He sure does love his Bible though. And those loose-fitting pants. You ever notice the way he sweats. I think he's so sexy. What do you think, Robin? Do you think Jimmy Swaggart is sexy?"

"Why do they scare you?" asks Sandra for the second time.

"Jimmy is the one that scares me the most. When he used to ask you to touch the TV I could sometimes feel my hand moving towards the screen."

"You?" says Robin.

"Why not me? I'm a sinner."

"But you want Jesus in your life?"

"No. I don't want Jesus in my life. But whenever Jimmy comes on I'm afraid I won't be able to stop myself. And if you touch the screen, it gets into you. You're lost."

"What gets into you?" asks Sandra.

"The rays. The power. I don't know. Whatever that stuff is that comes out of the television. That's why you're not supposed to sit too close to it."

When she is tired of cards, Sandra says, "Bob, get the camera." It is a Polaroid. Bob, who usually complains about having his photo taken, only requires a little prompting to pose in front of the tree with Cathy. They pass the camera around and Cathy takes one of Robin and Sandra arm in arm in front of the fireplace. Sandra poses Cathy and Robin on the couch, his arm over her shoulders. It is the same couch where she took the picture of Robin and Christopher two Christmases ago. Cathy kisses Robin on the cheek right after the flash. Sandra says, do that again, and takes one of the girl kissing her son.

Then Robin takes the camera and follows his mother

around the house. His mother by the fire. His mother in the kitchen. He doesn't, Bob notes, take one of his fiancée.

When she finally gets to bed Sandra can't sleep. She tries reading but she is too fidgety. She can't concentrate. She has hoped for this moment for so long. Now that it is here she feels uncomfortable. There is nothing wrong with the girl. She seems nice enough. A little soft perhaps, cowlike, but not fat, and attractive in her own way. She seems to have her head screwed on. She owns her condominium. Talked about her investment broker. How many single twenty-seven-year-old women could do that? Bob certainly liked her. Is that it? Is she jealous of the way her husband seems to be enjoying the girl? She didn't feel jealous. She had never been jealous of Robin's friends before. When he brought Christopher home she had liked that. But this wasn't the same, was it? Why was she feeling so sad? That's it. She feels sad. She feels like crying. She gets up and goes to the bathroom and stares in the mirror. She looks so old. So tired.

She falls asleep wondering if it is true that people can be saved by touching their television screens.

Christmas morning without children lacks urgency. It feels formal—like they are following rules. They wait until after breakfast to open their presents. Sandra has wrapped a toaster oven and a flannel nightie with rows of pink flowers for Cathy. She glances at her son on the couch and in the morning sun notices that his hair, which he still wears short, is beginning to thin in front. He is a handsome boy, she thinks. His moustache neatly trimmed. The collar of his pyjamas carefully folded over his silk robe. As usual he is wearing cologne. She remembers him as a little boy running into her bedroom on Christmas morning—bursting to get at his presents. Even he is old now.

She has given Robin some bed linen. Egyptian cotton. Three-hundred thread count.

"Perfect," he says. "Perfect." Means it.

She is opening one of his presents to her. It is wrapped in expensive foil paper. She opens it carefully, trying to save the paper, thinking as she opens it how good it is to have her son home. He has given her a new tablecloth. Linen damask. Burgundy. You can't beat a really good linen. Why doesn't her husband understand these things. She can't talk to Bob about flatware or crystal. Bob doesn't care about those sort of things.

Before lunch Sandra begins to work on dinner. She is roasting red bell peppers for a purée that she is going to serve with the green beans.

Cathy says, "Can I help?"

Sandra shows her how to skin the peppers. When she finishes she shows her how she likes the beans sliced.

"I've never seen them like this," says Cathy. "What's the point?"

Sandra doesn't know what the point is. She has always Frenched her beans. That is what her mother did.

"It looks nice, I guess," she says.

It is the first time they have been alone. Sandra wants to ask about Robin. She always learns important things about her son from his friends. But this time she doesn't know how to begin. This is different. His friends have always been boys. This is a girl. She feels that she should be careful. She shouldn't ask anything surreptitious or confusing. *Where did that come from? Who didn't she want to confuse?*

Cathy can feel the questions gathering in the kitchen like a summer storm. She is used to meeting people where they want to be met. Telling them what they want to hear. It is something she is good at. She has thought a lot about this. She has it all planned. She explained it to Robin in the car.

"Tell them I live in Vancouver," she said. "Or they'll want to see me in Toronto."

"What do you do?" he asked.

"What do you mean what do I do?"

"If they ask me what you do. What do I tell them you do?"

"Oh," she said. "What do I do?" She didn't even pause. "I teach German."

"A teacher?"

"For a language school."

She has created a world for herself. After they get

married she might keep working or she might go back to school. Get an MA in languages. Her father was a professor. He died in a car accident during her last year of high school. Her mother was driving the car.

Her mother remarried. To a man Cathy doesn't like. She hates him, in fact. He drinks. He hits her mother. Once he hit Cathy. She doesn't see her mother any more. That way, Cathy explained, if his parents asked to meet her parents, they could get around it. She could have a sister if he wanted.

"Do you think I should have a sister?"

"Up to you," said Robin.

"No. No," she said, playful now. "You decide."

"A sister," he said, trying it out. "A sister would be nice."

"OK. My sister is Rosic. OK?"

"Rosie?"

"Yeah. Rosie. But you haven't met her yet."

She is ready with all this. With Rosie, and her dead father and with stories about her dog and her best friend. She is anxious to try them out. What she isn't ready for are the questions about Robin. She hasn't planned on that.

"He's fine," she says, feeling her way carefully.

She tries to swing the conversation back onto ground where she is more comfortable. "He is very sweet to me."

She holds up the ring.

"He gave this to me," she says, "in a restaurant." She

is making this up on the spot. "A fancy place. An Italian place. They brought me my dessert, tartufo, and the ring was on top. On top of the ice cream."

Sandra is smiling. She looks over from the counter where she is chopping cashews for the stuffing. "You are doing a lovely job, dear," she says.

Sandra means a lovely job on the beans. Cathy thinks she means the stories she is telling.

"One Friday," she says, "he picked me up after work and we drove to Seattle. We had dinner in the tower. In the restaurant that spins?"

"He ordered Champagne," she says. "We laughed and laughed."

The beans are done. She goes into the living-room and turns on the television.

⊠ ⊠ ⊠

Sandra sets the dinner table with her new burgundy linen. She and Robin dominate the meal. Laughing, gossiping about her friends. Elise is doing her hair, she says. Elise? says Robin. The old bag. Bob and Cathy mostly listen. Talk a little about television. Find out that they both like "Jeopardy."

The next evening Sandra and Bob are invited to the Petersons' for drinks. Robin and Cathy stay home—alone for the first time since the drive up. Robin is reading on the couch.

Cathy sits beside him.

"How long will they be gone?"

"Two hours," he says. "Maybe three."

She touches his forehead.

"What do you like?" she asks. "Is there something you like? We could have our own party." She was trying to be nice. Trying to give him his money's worth.

He said, "No, I'm reading. I don't want to party. I want to be alone."

She knew he wasn't reading. She had been watching him. He was looking at the book but he hadn't turned a page in fifteen minutes.

* * *

Coming home from the Petersons' Sandra says, "Why did you want to leave so early? What was the big hurry?"

"No big hurry," says Bob.

The lights of the car ricochet along the snow piled at the edge of the lake road. It is dark. The banks of snow look hard and icy.

"You couldn't wait to get out of there. What's the hurry? You want to get back to the girl?"

"What?" he said. "What do you mean by that?"

"You know what I mean." She turns and looks out the window. Bob doesn't want to take this any further. Doesn't want to push them into something that will take days to come back from.

When they park the car in the driveway she tries again.

"Hurry up and get inside. She's waiting for you."

He stops, turns, and looks at her belligerently. As if she is a stranger who has bumped him deliberately. As if he is daring her to hit him again.

"Can't you see something's wrong?" she says. She means with the girl.

"What are you talking about?"

"You know what I'm talking about."

"No, I don't know what you're talking about and I am not in a hurry to see her. I am trying to be civil to her. Which is a lot more than you are to me."

"You are trying to be civil to her," says Sandra, mincing the words.

"What is the matter with you, Sandra? You're jealous of her? Sometimes..." He doesn't finish the sentence.

"Is that what you think, Bob? That's what you think. You wouldn't know a bus if it ran over you. You think I want to have him all to myself. That's what you think THIS is?"

"I don't know what this is Sandra. And no, that's not what I think. I don't think you want to mother Robin. You know what I think? I think you want Robin to mother you."

He has spoken a truth so close to the bone yet so far from their conscious understanding that she does not know what to say. Only that she feels enraged.

For the second time in their marriage she slaps her husband across the face.

"Merry Christmas," he says coldly, and walks into the house.

❖ ❖ ❖

Two years from now—Bob, dead of a heart attack, Robin, dead too—Sandra will think of this weekend often.

"I knew," she will say. And she did. She knew. Most of it. She had always known.

Sometimes, however, when the truth is staring you in the face, you rearrange what you know into patterns that you can believe. Years later Sandra will wonder how she did that.

"You don't do it," her friend Elise will say. "Your mind does it for you."

She came to think of that Christmas as one of the great accomplishments of her life.

I knew, but I let him have his way. I gave him that.

Sometimes she saw her complicity as an act of great courage. Other times as cowardice.

❖ ❖ ❖

That January, however, she still believed that it could be true. That her son *was* going to marry this girl who had spent Christmas with them. After Robin returned west, and she and Bob to the city, Sandra bought a pewter frame at Birks and framed the Polaroid of Robin and Cathy on the couch—the one in which Cathy was kissing Robin on the cheek. Even after Robin had died, after she knew they weren't really engaged, she kept the picture on a table in the living-room with a cluster of other photos. She liked to look at it when she felt melancholy. She thought of the afternoon she and the girl had fixed Christmas dinner together. She remembered the night they played charades. Bob and the girl were on the same team. She would like to see her again. Maybe go to lunch or something. But none of Robin's friends knew her, could tell her who she was.

On a sunny afternoon that same January, while he was visiting a customer in Kelowna, Robin remembered the engagement ring. It had cost $750. He had planned to return it when he got home. But he had forgotten to ask for it. On the drive back to the city he and Cathy had got drunk. She told him about her father.

"I used to think it was the only way I could get his attention," she said. "One day, afterwards, he rolled over and went to sleep. And I thought, I can't even get his attention like this. That's when I left home."

Robin told her about Christopher and about Bob Jones, the seminar leader. About the men he picked up in the coffee shops on Davie Street. About the time he was beaten up.

They said goodbye like friends. He was going to ask her phone number. But he felt awkward. Didn't want her to say no. Forgot about the ring.

He pulled out his Day-Timer and scribbled the word "ring" on the top of the page. He wasn't back in the office until Monday.

He called the number of the escort service he had used when he booked Cathy. He had chosen it from a page of ads in a weekly newspaper.

I want someone around twenty-five, he had said. Someone who has finished school. I don't want to sleep with her. I want to introduce her to my parents. As if she was my girlfriend. She has to be smart and look like she has been to college or something. And nice looking.

We have a someone, the woman said. A girl who goes to school in the mornings. Studies languages. She is a very nice young lady.

The number was disconnected.

She had said that her family name was Dietrich. Cathy Dietrich. Robin did not know if she was telling the truth. Surely she wouldn't use her real name?

He phoned information in Toronto and asked if they had any listings for Cathy Dietrich.

The lady said, "Kathy 'K' or Cathy 'C'?"

"I'm not sure," he said.

There were three K. Dietrichs.

And two "C's."

One of the "Cs" was unlisted.

That's her, he thought.

He thought of paying a private detective to get her number. Decided to let it go. She would have sold the ring anyway. What was the point? Wondered sometimes if her father really was a teacher. If he drank. If any of the things she told him driving back to Toronto were true.

It would have pleased him to know that she was the C. Dietrich in the book. That her name was Cathy. That she didn't sell the ring.

She was wearing it the afternoon she met her mother, for lunch at a restaurant on Church Street. It was the same January. It was the first time she had called her mother in over a year. The first time they had met for two years.

"I'm engaged," she said, holding her hand out. "His name is Robin, he works in Vancouver. I have a picture."

MAKE MONEY!
GET PRIZES!

he Sea-Monkey arrived on a Monday in June. They came surface mail from New York City, and depending on how you chose to measure it, took anywhere between forty years and two weeks in transit. If you *had* to be exact about it, two months would be the best estimate, for the die was cast the afternoon in April when Dave went for a walk along Queen Street and stumbled into a place called FUN-O-RAMA. When he got home he was bursting to tell his wife about it.

"I spent an hour there," he said. "It's only a hole in the wall but it's a great one. It's like walking into a comic book."

Morley was cooking supper. She said, "I've got to go to a library meeting tonight."

Then she said, "That's why I'm getting this pimple on the side of my nose."

Dave said, "They had everything. Strip pens. Exploding matches. I bought a deck of cards."

Dave had bought the FAMOUS VIEWS OF THE WORLD CARD DECK!

"Dracula's Castle," he said, holding up the four of clubs.

"Nice," said Morley.

271

Then she said, "Call the kids."

Then she said, "I thought there would be a time between pimples and wrinkles when I'd have a decent complexion. I knew I'd get wrinkles. But I never thought I'd have wrinkles and pimples at the same time."

Dave said, "Tiger Balm Garden, Hong Kong."

Then he said, "It's not that bad. You can hardly see it."

Morley said, "Right."

▣ ▣ ▣

A week later Dave spotted a small ad in the back of *Harper's* magazine.

SEND AWAY FOR STUPID STUFF
Free catalogue—$2

He sent the two dollars. The catalogue arrived a week and a half later. It was from Archie McPhee's Toy Store and Espresso Tiki Hut, Seattle, USA.

On the inside cover, opposite the table of contents, the catalogue posed a question Dave could not answer.

WHY LIVE ONE MORE DAY WITHOUT
AN INFLATABLE MUMMY?

He stayed up late filling out an order form. He was surprised when he added it up to find he had spent $147. American.

"One hundred and forty-seven dollars?" said Morley. "What did you get?"

"Wait," said Dave. "Wait and see."

◪ ◪ ◪

Dave's stuff arrived two weeks later. It was shipped in a cardboard carton labelled "Refrigerated Squid." He opened it after supper. This is what was in the box:

—two six-inch RUBBER SEA ALIENS! They were attached to elastic strings and were, more or less as the catalogue promised, "rubbery and strange."

—one life-sized RUBBER BRAIN.

—one bag of twelve assorted "pinkish slightly glowing" RUBBER BODY ORGANS: Heart! Lungs! Kidney! Pancreas and its relations!

—one faintly glowing RUBBER EYEBALL.

—one SHROUD OF TURIN-JESUS 3D CARD—"the portrait of Jesus is replaced by an 'Incredible' likeness of the reputed burial shroud."

—one DOGS PLAYING POKER! tapestry.

"This is great," said Dave, holding the tapestry up.

"I don't get it," said his daughter, Stephanie. "It's ugly."

—one GORILLAS EATING BANANAS KEY RING.

—one GLOW SQUID.

"What are you going to do with a glow squid?" asked Morley.

"The freezer light is broken," said Dave. "I thought we could keep it in the freezer."

—one small rubber DANGLING BAT.

—one rubber MOUSE KEY RING.

"This is the lizard," said Dave holding up the rubber Australian frilled lizard.

"There was a letter in the catalogue from a man in Texas who uses one of these babies in his bathroom. He keeps his toothbrush in its mouth and his comb back here. See."

"Cool," said Sam.

"This is stupid," said Stephanie.

"Rubber ants," said Sam. "There's a bag of rubber ants."

"Roaches," said Dave. "Those are rubber roaches."

"Cool," said Sam. "This is cool, Dad."

Sam was seven years old.

"Why do we need a rubber frog?" asked Morley.

"For the bathtub," said Dave. He was sitting on the living-room floor with his stuff spread around him like a boy at Christmas. "It's a squirt frog. It was supposed to come with evolving tadpoles. Are the tadpoles there?" Dave was pawing through the packaging. "And a book with metamorphosis facts. There was supposed to be a book. Three dollars and seventy-five cents for the whole package.

"Here," said Dave. "Everyone gets one of these. Put them on."

Dave was holding four pairs of plastic glasses—each one came with a rubber nose, a fake moustache and fake eyebrows.

"Look, he said, putting his glasses on, "Groucho Marx."

Dave stood up. He pretended he was smoking a cigar.

He said, "Time flies like an arrow. Fruit flies like a banana. Nyah, nyah, nyah."

Stephanie had peeled the bill of lading off the box. "This stuff cost $147. How come Daddy is allowed to spend $147 on stuff like this and I can't get a pair of Docs? Docs don't cost $147. This isn't fair. We don't need this stuff. What are we going to do with a rubber brain? I *need* Docs."

She got up and left the three of them sitting in the living-room wearing their plastic glasses.

Dave felt angry. Then he felt stupid.

That night as they were going to bed Dave said to Morley, "That made me sad."

"Not sad enough," said Morley.

"I feel sad," said Dave.

He was lying on the bed with his hands folded under his head.

"I was thinking about all the stuff you saw in comics when I was a kid. X-RAY GLASSES. ITCHING POWDER. I thought we could have fun with a box of junk like that. Maybe she's right. It *is* stupid. It's supposed to be stupid. But not stupid stupid. Maybe we should just get her the Docs."

"Maybe," said Morley.

Dave sat up.

"You know what I forgot all about?" he said. "The weight-gain ads."

"You mean the weight-loss ads," said Morley.

"No," said Dave. "Weight-*gain*. Muscle-building."

"Oh," said Morley. "The 98-pound weakling."

"Those ads were written for me," said Dave.

Morley was standing by her bureau, her head tipped forward, her hair covering her face, brushing the day out.

"You're supposed to do this one hundred times," she said. "Who has time for that?" She dropped her brush onto her bureau.

Dave said, "Remember the other day you were talking about your face? Remember you said you never thought you would have pimples and wrinkles at the same time? It's like that with my body."

Morley was standing in the middle of the bedroom, looking around, as if she had lost something.

Dave said, "I always thought I was too skinny. I wouldn't wear shorts in the summer. I hated going swimming. Those ads were an affirmation of everything I thought about myself."

Morley said, "Have you seen my book? Go on."

"I was the before shot. My elbows were the biggest part of my arms. My legs were spindly. I was the chicken-chested weakling."

"Toothpick arms?" said Morley, as she cruised around the bedroom.

"The original muscle-starved string-bean," said Dave.

"Girls made fun of you behind your back?" said Morley, lifting a sweater off the floor and peering underneath it.

"Exactly," said Dave.

Morley said, "How could I lose a book I only read in bed?"

Dave said, "You always said you loved tall skinny men."

"Yup," said Morley. "I give up." She flopped onto the bed. "And you didn't believe me."

"Couldn't believe you. Couldn't. Not even in principle. I thought it was just words. I thought you were just saying it."

"I married you didn't I?"

"Yeah. I know."

"I *love* your body."

"Yeah, yeah."

"I *love* your skinny legs."

She snuggled up beside her husband. He sat up. He wasn't finished.

"One night we were at a party. And there was this tall skinny guy there. Do you remember this? He was dressed all in black. He looked like Ichabah Crane. Very intense. And I thought, he doesn't look so bad. In fact I thought he looked…great. I was still hung up about my legs, but skinny, in principle, wasn't so bad any more."

"Icha*bod.*"

"What?"

"It's Icha*bod.* Icha*bod* Crane. You said Ichabah."

"Whatever. You know when that happened? Two years ago. When I was forty-five years old. And I didn't weigh 135 pounds any more. I was pushing 170 and it was all on my stomach.

"Suddenly I'm forty-five years old and I have the body that I always swore I wouldn't have. I have a pot goddamn it. So where's the part without pimples. Where was I when that was happening?"

Morley said, "Show me your pot. I *love* your pot."

Dave said, "I'm serious."

Morley sat up. "Oh," she said. All concerned. "He's *serious.*"

Dave said, "Forget it. I don't know why I am telling

you this. This has nothing to do with anything. Do you
think we should get her the Docs?"

⊠ ⊠ ⊠

Stephanie came home on Saturday afternoon in a new
pair of Doc Marten's. She had bought them with her
own money.

"Aren't they cool, Daddy?"

"They look heavy."

"They're the BEST," said Stephanie.

"Aren't they hot?" said Morley, walking into the
kitchen.

"It used to be an insult," said Dave.

"What?" said Morley.

"Army boots," said Dave. "Your mother wears army
boots."

Stephanie sat down at the table and put her feet up
on a chair so she could admire her new shoes. The
Archie McPhee catalogue was under a plant on the
table in front of her. She picked it up and began leafing
through it.

"Hey," she said. "We should get the Sea-Monkeys."

Dave said, "I thought you didn't like that stuff."

Stephanie said, "The stuff *you* got. Sea-Monkeys are
cool."

She didn't know that Dave had wanted Sea-Monkeys
most of his life. He could still visualize the ads that ran

on the back pages of the comic books he used to buy when he was a boy. The water-colour painting of the Sea-Monkey family with their little Sea-Monkey crowns in place and their monkey castle in the background. The mom and the dad and the two kids peering at the fish bowl and the Sea-Monkeys swimming around.

Just ADD water—that's ALL!
in ONE SECOND your
AMAZING Sea-Monkeys actually
COME TO LIFE.
ONLY $1.25 to own a
BOWLFUL OF HAPPINESS.

What Dave wanted to know when he was a boy, what he still wanted to know, was would they really come to life? Or were they just something that looked alive? He knew they wouldn't look the way they looked in the comic book. The mother Sea-Monkey was wearing lipstick. He knew that couldn't be right.

As a boy the ad had crippled him. He had obsessed on Sea-Monkeys and promised himself he was going to *do it!* They only cost a dollar twenty-five. That wasn't much money—even back then. But he never sent for them. He always pulled up short. And it made him feel stupid—stupid that he couldn't enter into the spirit of the thing—like at a carnival. You know she isn't going to be a MONKEY WOMAN! but you pay the buck anyway—so you can see how they have structured the lie. It's not about MONKEY WOMAN! It's about the use of language, and hyperbole. It's a game of wink and nudge and...and he was too afraid of appearing gullible to play along. He hated himself because of it.

◙ ◙ ◙

Dave and Stephanie sent away for the Sea-Monkeys together. Stephanie filled out the form—Dave paid. They went for all the gimmicks. For the Sea-Pendant that you could put the Sea-Monkeys in and wear around your neck. The Sea-Medic which was a powder you gave them if they got the dreaded Black Spot Disease. The Sea-Monkey Treats and the Jumbo Aquarium with the flashing light. They arrived two weeks later in a brown paper package the size of a large box of cereal.

They made a big production of it. In the kitchen after dinner. Like it was a big joke.

"Here we go," said Dave, dumping the powder into the aquarium. "Life."

Dave was joking but not completely—part of him actually felt liberated, released. He was completing something.

"I'm creating life," he said.

They kept the Sea-Monkeys in the kitchen. The aquarium had a magnifier on the side. Even through the magnifier the Sea-Monkeys didn't look like much. They looked like black smudges—like microscopic finishing nails.

"Actually," said Dave to Sam one evening, "they're not monkeys. They're some kind of shrimp. They're hardly on the evolutionary scale. Maybe slightly above amoebas."

But they had one thing going for them. They had perpetual life.

In July Morley and Dave rented a cottage in Muskoka and while they were gone the aquarium dried out and when they came home all that was left of the Sea-Monkeys was a little pile of white crystals. Like a pile of salt. Dave added water and some of the instant life powder—it was a catalyst or a water purifier or something—and the shrimp came back to life.

"Life," he said. "Incredible."

◫ ◫ ◫

One night in August Morley was on her way to the fridge when she bent down to pick up one of the rubber roaches that was lying on the kitchen floor. As her shadow crossed over it the roach scurried under the stove. Morley gasped and jumped back.

She called Dave.

Dave said, "We should spray."

He bought some stuff and they sprayed on the weekend. Some of the spray must have got into the aquarium—just traces of it—no one thought to cover it—and the Sea-Monkeys grew tails.

By the end of the week they had a bowlful of

mutant Sea-Monkeys. They couldn't swim because of the weight of the tails; so they sank and drowned. And that was the end of them.

⊠ ⊠ ⊠

Stephanie organized the funeral. She dressed Sam in black and made them both earrings out of the rubber roaches. She put the Sea-Monkeys on a Kleenex bed in a cereal box. Then she called Dave.

"Trust me, Daddy," she said as he peered at the cardboard casket. "They're all there."

They buried them by candlelight in the backyard.

When they started they were horsing around, making it campy and mock serious, but when Stephanie started to drop dirt on the box, saying, "Monkey to monkey; powder to dust," the ceremony suddenly turned serious.

They all stood there without saying a word while Sam filled up the grave.

When there was no reason to stand there any longer Dave said, "Well. That's that."

Later, when the kids were in bed, he said, "That's the problem with funerals. They all sort of blend together and become one big funeral. Remember when we buried the pig?"

"What?" said Morley.

"The guinea pig," said Dave.

"Oh."

Morley was crying.

"I'm sorry," she said. "It's stupid."

She was thinking about her father.

Dave said, "Come here."

She didn't come. He went to her.

Wrapped his arms around her.

Held her.

"Sorry," he said. "Sorry."